The Ideals
of Adelia

The Ideals
of Adelia

Hannah G. Attridge

gatekeeper press™

Columbus, Ohio

The Ideals of Adelia

Published by Gatekeeper Press
2167 Stringtown Rd, Suite 109
Columbus, OH 43123-2989
www.GatekeeperPress.com

Library of Congress Control Number: 2021946315

ISBN (paperback): 9781662919329
eISBN: 9781662919336

For the exceptional individuals in my life,

who encouraged me

while I was creating this story.

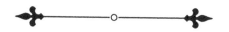

Chapter 1

The freshly inked envelope was resting on the table, sunlight flickering across its secure scarlet seal, highlighting the well-defined initial A embedded in the hardened wax. It seemed to taunt me, asking me to open it secretly. I purged the thought the moment it entered my mind. I knew very well it was not my place to open correspondence that was addressed to my uncle and aunt.

I flipped over the letter to examine it more closely. It read in bold black ink, "To Mr. and Mrs. Richard Hadlee and Miss Adelia Hadlee". It was addressed from the Ansley's, which made my heart skip a beat. I thought of all the possibilities of why they would send us written correspondence through the local post. An invitation to a ball seemed the most logical explanation, and I was eager to open it and confirm my suspicions. I peered out the window to see if the carriage was back yet. My aunt and uncle had left earlier this afternoon to visit their friends, the Barlow's, for tea. Mr. and Mrs. Barlow live a few miles up the road from our home. Admittedly, I feigned a headache coming on to avoid going with them. I love the Barlow's, as they are old family friends, but conversation with the two of them can get dull at times.

I sighed and settled back down into the weathered armchair by the window. There was still no sign of their return, and my fingers were twitching to open the envelope! I focused my attention back on my needlepoint to try and distract myself. I stared dismally at my handiwork, which greatly resembled much of nothing. This design was supposed to turn into a lovely vase of flowers, but I was failing miserably at the craft. I gingerly set my disappointing creation down on the side table next to the chair, as I had quickly lost interest in pursuing craft activities at this moment.

I started to dreamily stare at the cherry trees that were blossoming in our garden. The pink flowers began opening as soon as April came and produced a divine presence on our grounds. My mind began to wander, and it settled on the subject of the Ansley's. Particularly the eldest Ansley son, Henry. I felt a tingle, then a flutteringly rush pass through my chest when I thought of his name. The Ansley's moved to our small coastal town, Hastings, from London this last winter. Our little community had been relatively unchanging before they arrived, but they seemed to usher in the bustle and energetic air of city life with their presence. They are fairly wealthy landowners apparently, and the parents decided to purchase a property here on the coast for a change of scenery. Mr. Matthew Ansley and Mrs. Rachel Ansley have three children. Clara is the youngest of the siblings being eighteen, Oliver is the middle child of two and twenty, and Henry is the oldest, being four and twenty. I am not sure if I can describe the feelings that I have developed for Henry, as they seem so strong at times. I still vividly remember seeing him at the first social dance that the Ansley's had attended in our town. I fully recall taking in his stately stature and pleasing countenance with my discreet and discerning eyes. His dark blonde hair, burnt umber eyes, and winning smile made my knees weak instantaneously. My feelings have grown stronger and ever steady since I first met him. My only vexation is that I am not sure what his opinion is regarding me. Of course, we were introduced shortly after the Ansley's arrived, but we have not had many conversations since then. Henry also seems to be a very mature and reticent person. That is why an invitation to a ball would be marvelous! There might be a chance that Henry and I could dance together or at least have a meaningful conversation to further our acquaintance.

A sharp knock at the front door drew me from my reverie. I looked up in confusion because I was not aware that we were expecting visitors. I heard Alice, our cook and housekeeper, open the door, say hello to someone, and then a dripping wet figure burst through the study door.

"Edith! What are you doing here?" I asked my good friend in utter confusion.

"Oh, Adelia!" She exclaimed, in between huffing, and puffing for air. "I ran all the way here when I heard the news. Oh, I feel as if I am going to faint! I must sit down."

She collapsed into my favorite pink plushy chair situated next to the fireplace. I shook my head in amusement at her dramatics. Edith Camden and I have known each other since we were five years of age. She is vivacious and outgoing, while I am more reserved and quieter at times. Whenever we are together, it seems as if we are always hatching plans for some sort of escapade. It did not surprise me that she had seemingly run all the way from her house, which is about ten minutes up the road, to tell me something important. "What news is there, Edith, that is so desperately urgent you ran in the rain to come and converse with me?" I finally asked.

"Only the most crucial news that we have been waiting for Adelia!" She exclaimed with a smile.

"Well? Are you going to keep me waiting for eternity, or are you going to tell me?" I demanded with exasperation. Edith loves being the teller of sensational gossip, and she equally enjoys drawing out the moment for exaggerated effect.

"My mother invited Ms. Whittington over for tea this afternoon and I was required to sit in, and as you know Ms. Whittington is only the biggest busybody in all of Hastings! Anyways, the conversation turned to social events of the season, and she mentioned that rumor has it the Ansley's are preparing to throw a ball at the beginning of May!" She squealed.

My breath caught at that statement. It most likely was an invitation in the envelope! "Did she say anything else?" I asked with eagerness.

"Well, listen closely, because this is the best part! It seems that they are eagerly trying to integrate their two sons, Henry and Oliver, into different social circles in hopes of them making marriage connections. Ms. Whittington filled us in on those details, and as she seems to have gotten close to Mrs. Rachel Ansley in recent months, it appears as if they are mostly accurate." Edith finished with a sigh. "Now we can only hope to get invited to their ball!"

"Edith, a letter came in the mail just this afternoon, addressed from the Ansley's! I think it might be an invitation for the ball!" I declared.

"Let me see it!" Edith requested with forceful insistence. I plucked the envelope and delivered it into her eager hands. "You have not opened it?" She asked with bewilderment.

"No, it came right after my uncle and aunt left for tea at the Barlow's. It has been agonizing me for almost an hour!" I admitted.

Edith swiftly ripped open the envelope and started rustling around for its contents. "Edith!" I shouted. "What are you doing? It is addressed to my uncle and aunt. I was waiting for them to come home before I opened it."

"Well, your name is on it too." She reasoned. "They will not mind. Do you want to see what is in it or not?" Curiosity got the best of me.

"Fine!" I said as I snatched the thick piece of paper from her hands. My heart leapt as I read over the words. It was an invitation!

April 23rd, 1857

Mrs. Rachel Ansley requests the honor of your presence for a formal evening dress ball on Saturday the second of May at half-past seven in the evening. To be held at the Ansley residence, Greenwood: 14 Cavendish Ave.

"I am so happy Edith!" I shrieked. "This is what I have been waiting for! I can just imagine being there in my best dress, maneuvering through the people in hopes of Henry noticing me. And what if he asks to dance with me? That would make me the happiest girl in the world." I sighed gleefully, imagining the possibilities.

"Well, I would be happy if my family gets invited. How come your invitation came already?" Edith pouted.

"Typically, I am not handed the mail, but as my aunt and uncle are out, Alice put today's post on the table when it was delivered. Maybe yours has not come yet?" I suggested.

"It could be possible. However, my father usually intercepts the mail as soon as it arrives at our house, so it may have already been delivered. I do hope you are right because I think it would be rather unfair if you got an invitation and I did not. I want to be there as badly as you do. I know you are madly in love with Henry Ansley, but I completely fancy his younger brother Oliver." Edith concluded with a dreamy look on her face.

"When did this develop?" I asked with surprise. Edith had not mentioned her feelings for Oliver to me yet.

"Oh, a little bit ago." She replied mysteriously with a sly look on her face.

"Why have we not discussed it before now?" I said incredulously.

"Because our conversations are usually spent talking about your intense admiration for Henry." She responded teasingly.

I blushed. "That may or may not be true." I said with some embarrassment. I do not think I had fully realized how much time I have spent talking about Henry with Edith. Reflecting on it made me feel a bit self-conscious.

"I kind of wanted to keep it to myself for some time." She continued. "It is fun to have a secret. Can you imagine if you married Henry and I married Oliver? We would be sisters-in-law!"

A sheepish smile crept across my face just pondering the thought of it. "It would be a dream come true!" I said sillily.

She laughed. "I must go home and find out if I have an invitation to the ball! If we both end up attending we will have to consult on each other's toilette to help one another get ready."

"Yes, that sounds delightful! I will see you soon." I said as I gave her an embrace to say goodbye. And just as quickly as she arrived, Edith flitted out the door and started down the path that led to her home. I smiled as I watched her from the window. She was truly such a dear person to me, always acting like almost a sister all these years. With me not having any siblings, Edith has filled that void with her bubbling personality and sincere friendship.

I glanced out to the window again at the sound of horse hooves clattering up the driveway. My aunt and uncle were back! I rushed outside to greet them. "Aunt Leah! Uncle Richard!" I called. "We have received an invitation!"

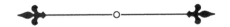

Chapter 2

I was sitting in the garden, overlooking a grassy meadow that rolled out behind our cottage. A pair of small skylarks kept darting back and forth from the pine trees where they resided. They were happily chirping and singing to each other, which made me smile. It was such a perfect day. I breathed in the smell of sweet flowers and dewy grass. April was almost over, and I had concluded that I was thoroughly enjoying spring. The weather appeared to be agreeable this season with the rain that would come some days, which helped the flowers and plants bloom, and the warm, radiant days that made me long for summer. It seemed to be a time of renewal, and my hopes and expectations were abounding. Aunt Leah agreed that a ball sounded like a splendid source of amusement, and Uncle Richard had consented, saying that we would accept the Ansley's invitation.

With my paintbrush poised in hand, I grazed the paper with a stroke of bright color. While I took in the view of my surroundings, I became transfixed with the honeysuckle plants that were growing up against the stone wall in the garden. I started to brush the paper back and forth with paint and a picture began forming in front of my eyes. The talent I possess in painting watercolor scenes makes up for the skill I lack with needlepoint.

After some time, I stood back and scrutinized my work. Being satisfied, I laid my paintbrushes aside and wiped my hands on my apron. I took a deep breath as I sat down on a bench near where I had set up my easel. Suddenly, falling footsteps and the playful chatter of voices in the distance disrupted the restful silence. I looked over curiously to see what or who was moving through the gently blowing grass. I was startled to see three figures walking through the field, up to where I was sitting in my garden. Even more terrifying was when I realized it was the Ansley siblings approaching! My stomach flipped when I caught sight of Henry walking behind his brother Oliver and sister Clara. I frantically started to tuck my curls that were sliding out of my hair pins behind my ears and untie the knot that held up my paint-splattered apron.

"Adelia!" Clara called and waved her hand. I smiled nervously and waved back. The Ansley's estate, Greenwood, was situated just up the hill from our cottage, named Cliffside. Past the meadow behind our house, a line of pine trees covers a sloping sandy cliff, creating a path down to the sparkling ocean.

I walked out past the garden gate to greet them. "Hello. This is a pleasant surprise." I said cautiously.

"Hello, Miss Hadlee." Oliver greeted me brightly. Henry acknowledged me with a perfect, shy smile.

"How are you, Adelia?" Clara asked eagerly.

"I am well. What brings you here?" I asked awkwardly. My tongue was not eager to obey my thoughts when I attempted to talk while Henry was standing four feet away, watching everything quietly.

"Mother wanted me to return Ms. Whittington's piano sheet music that she had borrowed for me. We were able to make copies of it at the printery shop of course, and she requested that I give back the originals in a timely fashion. Mother did not want me going alone, so we all thought it would be nice to take a walk outside." Clara explained swiftly. "When we finished visiting with Ms. Whittington,

I wanted to walk down the hill through the wildflowers, and then I saw you in the garden and we decided to come over and say hello!"

I nodded understandingly. "Thank you for coming by. I was occupied with practicing my watercolor painting, but you caught me right as I had finished."

"I did not know you painted!" Clara exclaimed. "May I see what you were working on?"

"Well, I am only an amateur, I do not think I am very...." Clara was not listening however and walked past me to where the easel was set up.

"Sorry, she can get excitable at times." Oliver said with a shrug as he and Henry followed her through the garden. I also walked over, anxious at all three of them, particularly Henry, looking at my work.

"Oh Adelia, this is lovely! You are incredibly talented!" Clara declared.

"This is very good indeed. Do you paint often?" Oliver asked.

"When I have time. I prefer to paint outside, especially now that the weather is favorable." I replied, scanning Henry's face for any hint of approval. He was still silent but continued to thoughtfully gaze at my artwork.

I centered my attention back on Clara. "Well, where are you off to now? Do you have to go back home?" I questioned.

Clara gazed expectedly at her older brothers. "I really want to take a walk down on the shoreline. Mother said we could be out for a little while if we stayed together and return home before tea. Can we go, Henry? Oliver? Please?" She implored while tilting her head, attempting to use a pouty facial expression to silently entreat her brothers into compliance.

Henry smiled at his sister's juvenile effort to make things go her way. "Yes, Clara. I think taking a walk would be a fine idea. Why don't you ask Miss Hadlee to join us?" He proposed. I jumped at the idea! Henry had just suggested that I go with them for a stroll! This truly was a good day!

"Oh yes! You should come, that would be delightful!" Clara said, exuberantly happy that things were going her way.

"Your aunt and uncle would be welcome to come as well." Oliver added.

"I would like that very much. Let me go into the house and see if they wish to accompany us." I said and hurried into the cottage to ask them.

My aunt and uncle both decided that exercise and fresh air would be a great idea and soon all six of us were walking down through the tall grass and past the sand dunes to the water. The weather in the coastal region always seemed a bit nippy with the wind and I was glad that I had grabbed a shawl from my room before we set out. My uncle and the Ansley young men were walking farther ahead of us, and I could hear them laughing every so often. My aunt and I were trying to establish a conversation with Clara.

"Adelia tells me you practice piano, Clara. What are some of your favorite pieces to play?" Aunt Leah inquired of her.

"My preference is Mendelssohn, I believe." She answered. "I am working on a particularly tricky piece right now of his that is beautiful to listen to. I like most composers though, my governess always had me working on multiple songs at once when I was younger."

I listened with interest. We had a small piano instrument that I could play to some extent. I never had a governess, and I did not go to a traditional school. My aunt was a teacher before she was married so she carried out my education. The additional skills I have come naturally or were taught to me by my aunt.

"That is impressive Clara. Mendelssohn's music can be complicated from what I remember." I said with genuine admiration

"Thank you, but you must know I was most impressed with your painting Adelia. I was taught watercolor by my governess, but I never could get the knack for it. That takes real skill. Who taught you?" She quizzed me.

Aunt Leah spoke up for me. "Adelia surprised us a few years ago when she brought out sketches that she had been drawing on her own with graphite. She took to painting just as naturally when we bought her paint supplies as a gift."

"Really? So, you learned on your own? I have never met someone who had art as a natural skill." She concluded.

We had reached the edge of the water line. The tide was drawn back into the ocean, and we could see all the bright carved shells and tiny sea creatures crawling through the sand.

"Some of these shells are so shiny! I want to find a few to take home!" Clara squealed as she ran forward through the tide searching for any object that caught her eye.

"I am going to catch up with Richard and walk with him." My aunt told me.

"Alright." I said with a smile. I stayed where I was and took in the sight of the ocean in front of me. The glinting blue water was rolling into white foamy waves that lapped onto the sand. I closed my eyes and breathed in the smell of salt and grass. The wind whipped through the air, rustling my skirt, and pushing my brunette locks against my face.

"It looks as if you certainly enjoy the beach." I heard a voice address me. I whirled around and saw that Henry had walked over to talk to me. My heartbeat quickened.

"I do, very much. I have lived here all my life. I do not think I could call any other place my home. How do you like it here?" I asked him, curious to see what he would say.

"It is different from London." Henry admitted. "I miss many friends and people that I know in the city. We used to visit here for holidays, but obviously, it seems that we will be here for a while."

"I would love to go someplace new for a change. I adore the coast and our cottage, but I long for new horizons and more excitement. When I was younger, I would gaze at books that had paintings of faraway countries and foreign cultures. I used to daydream that I could wish myself away to those unknown places." I confided to him.

"I can understand that. I would pretend to be studying arithmetic in school while reading and looking at atlases." Henry said with a laugh. "You have never been to the city though? You might like it. It is a different change of pace."

"Hopefully, I will someday. I would love to see this beloved London of yours." I said in a playful tone. "Will you be returning soon?"

"I am not sure. I enjoy residing here in Hastings; it is more peaceful and relaxed. But I feel as if I have mounting pressure from my parents being their oldest son. I am well past the age of matrimony, and they keep talking of marriage. I am not opposed to

having a partner of course, but I want it to be with the right person."
He answered me while looking into my eyes. It was all I could do to
nod in understanding. His stare took my breath away. One minute
we were talking about traveling and then the next he was talking of
marriage!

"Those are my sentiments and thoughts exactly." I agreed with
him. Henry nodded and stepped closer to me. He then reached into
his pocket and pulled out a few smooth shells and agates.

"I found these further down in the sand. Would you like them?"
He asked me with his bashful smile. He dropped them gently into
my hand.

"Thank you." I said timidly, as I closed my fingers around his
small gift.

"Your painting was quite good, by the way. You have a natural
talent." He continued with praise. I felt heat creep up my face and I
am sure my cheeks were glowing. Henry now took out his pocket
watch and looked at the time. "We must be getting home. It is half
an hour until tea." He stated while beckoning Oliver and Clara over
with a wave.

"This was pleasant. Thank you for asking us to come with you."
I said, grateful to have had this small outing in close company with
him.

"It was very agreeable. I am glad you came." He responded
smoothly. Clara and Oliver were upon us now. My aunt and uncle
were walking over as well. Clara's blonde hair was flying with the
wind and her cheeks were flushed from jogging in the sand.

"Oh, we have to go, don't we?" She asked sadly. "It was fun though!
Thank you for coming Adelia!" She exclaimed while embracing me

with a hug. "I do not have many friends in Hastings yet, and it is a pleasure to be in your company."

"I enjoy spending time with you too, Clara." I sincerely told her.

"You and your aunt will have to come for tea sometime. It would be a delight!" She offered.

"That would be lovely. We would be happy to come." Aunt Leah replied.

"It was nice talking with you young men." Uncle Richard said while shaking their hands.

"We look forward to seeing you at the ball next week." Henry said while looking directly at my face. My breath caught in my throat as we locked eyes.

"Yes, that will be most exciting. See you then." My aunt replied.

"Goodbye for now." I heard myself barely utter. I felt overstrung with anxiety when I was around Henry. He made me so nervous! I watched as Henry, Oliver, and Clara climbed back up the path through the sand dunes and disappeared into the tree line. I sighed and turned back around towards my aunt and uncle. They were both watching me with amused expressions on their faces.

"What? What is it?" I asked with trepidation.

My aunt gave out a giggle as she pulled me close. "Adelia, do you think I have not noticed your regard for Henry? Your eyes resemble glistening stars in a night sky when he is around you." I blushed for probably the eighth time in that hour.

"So, you have observed that?" I said hesitantly. I felt embarrassed that my behavior was so noticeable.

"Only because I know my niece so well." She reassured me. "Let us get on home for tea and I want to talk about it some more with you."

"Alright." I said somewhat excited to talk about my feelings with someone of the female persuasion, and on the other hand a bit fearful about what she would have to say to me.

Thirty minutes later, my aunt and I were facing each other in the sitting room of our cottage with teacups poised in hand. A plate of biscuits and crumpets sat to the right of our chairs waiting to be consumed. My uncle had decided that he was not in want of tea and had retired to the study until our supper. I quietly sipped on my tea, hesitant to start the conversation.

"Miss Adelia? I wish to know, when did Mr. Henry Ansley first catch your eye?" Aunt Leah inquired with a teasing formality as she grabbed a flaky biscuit and began slathering the pastry with the delicious, slippery jam.

"Well Aunt Leah, if I think back to the exact day and time, it would most definitively have to be when I saw him at the community dance back in December." I answered with a happy smile spreading across my face. I could not help it, thinking of that memory made me almost completely turn into a foolish little girl! The recollection came back to me as easily as if it had happened last week. I was walking by a doorway at the hall on my way to find Edith, and Henry Ansley's presence struck me to the core. He was standing in that entry, animatedly talking to another young man, and his whole countenance seemed luminescent.

"The dance in December?" My aunt inquired with eyebrows upturned. "That was a few months back and the Ansley's had barely been here a month."

"It was instantaneous." I explained quickly and stuffed a crumpet in my mouth.

My aunt quietly laughed again and took a sip from her teacup. "What did you notice about him that so instantaneously caught your eye?"

"His face was beautiful Aunt Leah!" I babbled out excitedly. "While he was talking with someone he smiled in his glowy way, and it sparked joy through my very being. Ever since then my feelings have seemed to have gotten deeper and stronger. However, by now with what I have said you must think that I am somewhat delusional."

"Of course not Adelia!" Aunt Leah reassured me. "If only you knew how many young men I liked when I was younger before I met Richard. It is normal to feel the way you feel for Henry."

I breathed a shaky sigh of relief. She understood me! "Thank you. It feels wonderful to not be teased about this. Edith and I end up goading each other about our attractions for the Ansley men. She is greatly enamored with Oliver apparently."

"Yes, that sounds like Edith. She wears her heart on her sleeve per se, so it is easy to tell when she likes a certain person." Aunt Leah said with a giggle. I laughed too. She was describing my dear friend perfectly.

"What we have said about her today, stays between us." I said jokingly.

"Of course." My aunt responded with her mischievous grin. "Back to our previous conversation about Henry, what else do you admire about him? Of course, he is handsome, I thought so myself when we first met the Ansley's, but what other qualities does he have that you find appealing?"

"He seems to be a more reserved person." I answered while thinking about certain things I have noticed while observing Henry.

"His maturity then?" Aunt Leah clarified.

"I suppose so. He seems different than the other men that I know. Young people can seem immature and fickle at social events. It is almost as if the young women would be completely happy and content to accept whichever man shows them any ounce of attention. And it seems that the men know it!" I purged my observations to her.

My aunt nodded in agreement. "It has always been like that. The men have the advantage over the women."

I agreed and continued. "But Henry seems different. He does not flirt with all the girls, and he stays on the sidelines most of the time with his family. I think he is special."

My aunt cleared her throat. "Well, that may or may not be true, Adelia. It does take time to get to know a person's true inner self."

I stiffened at her remark. "Yes, I do know that. I am getting to know him, Aunt Leah. I actually had a somewhat meaningful conversation with him earlier today."

"I understand that we have talked about this before, but I guess what I am trying to convey is that you are young and unfortunately will not go into your marriage union with a great fortune."

What she was saying was beginning to make me feel unsettled. "I will be one and twenty in October." I huffed.

"But you are an inexperienced young woman. And the problem with pining away for Henry is that the Ansley's do have more money than us and they might be encouraging him as their oldest son to make a romantic connection with a lady who can match his wealth." My aunt tried to tell me.

I did not want to listen to her anymore. "The way he looks at me is enough to keep my hope lingering. I feel as if we have the beginnings of a sincere connection!"

"I just want you to be careful. I am concerned about the potential of you getting hurt. I had my share of heartbreak when I was young and single." She replied.

I had to stop the urge to roll my eyes. I felt that I had heard her say this several times before. "Well, I think I know what I am doing, and it is my life, however young I may be." I responded shrewishly. I was frustrated with her projecting her life experiences onto me.

My aunt looked at me for a moment and finally sighed. "Of course, you do, Adelia. You have always been a determined person. You inherited that particular quality from your mother."

I smiled at that. "She really was so very stubborn?" I inquired.

"Yes… Yes, she was indeed! I was the older sister, so I felt that I had to act with proper decorum and fall in line. However, your mother, Jolee, being the younger daughter, was uninhibited around all types of people. When she set her heart upon something, nothing would stand in her way. That is why, when she met your father, I knew she had succumbed to his affections. It did not matter that he was poorer than she was or that our father did not approve of him. She loved him with her whole heart. I see in your eyes the same resolve that Jolee had when it came to your father."

My heart warmed to hear expressions about my parents. I held on to any little snippets of information that I could get, for I did not remember much about my mother and father. I suddenly felt guilty for rebuffing my aunt's concerns. "Thank you for talking to me, and I am sorry if I came across as ungracious. I just really like Henry and the way he makes me feel. I hope it will work out for us." I said with dark doubts creeping into the back of my mind.

"Oh Adelia, it will be alright. Everything seems to work out eventually, for better or for worse. Come and give me a hug and then our tea party will have to be over. I must go pop into the kitchen and see what Alice is cooking up for dinner." She told me while enveloping me with her comforting arms.

I embraced her and watched as she left the room. I was extremely grateful to Aunt Leah for being loving and motherly to me throughout the years. I was irked by her advice, however. I did not want to listen or give in to voices that told me it was not reasonable to imagine a future with Henry.

These thoughts muddled through my mind the rest of the evening. As I went to bed that night, I kept asking myself how something that feels so wonderful could have the potential to turn into a devastating situation. The thought of Henry showing attention to another girl made my heart wrench violently in my chest.

After tossing and turning for several hours, I sat up in my bed and glanced around my room. There was no hope that I was going to get any restorative sleep that night. It was hard for me to not dwell on the possibility that Henry had a girl who he was actively pursuing. He even said that he missed people that he knows in the city. Maybe a lady in London has already stolen his heart!

I got up and lit the candle on my nightstand. The warm light of the flame started making shadows dance across the corners of my wall. I began to pace around my room anxiously, imagining a mystery girl that held the key to Henry's heart. She would be beguiling with silky fair hair and have dazzling eyes with long lashes that she would batt at him to make his heart flutter. He would caress her hands and she would lift her rosy lips to kiss his face. It would be a scene reminiscent of the gothic novels that Aunt Leah had strictly forbidden me to read, but I had secretly snuck from Edith for years.

I vigorously shook my head in hopes of erasing this distressing image from my thoughts. It was upsetting to dwell on it any longer. I caught a glimpse of myself in my dressing table mirror. Large green eyes stared back at me. My hair was escaping from my braid and turning into a flyaway frizzy mess. I could never seem to figure out how to tame my natural curls so that they could be used to my advantage. I smoothed my hands down my nightgown to examine my torso. Ever since being introduced to the pure torture of a corset as a young woman, I have worried about maintaining a slim figure. My body seems determined to project curves, however. My complexion frustrates me as well, with the freckles that are splattered across my cheeks and the occasional red bump that appears on my chin.

I sighed wearily as exhaustion started to spread through my bones like water seeping into the parched ground. My tired gaze focused on the tiny shells that Henry had given me earlier. They were resting on my bookshelf next to all my beloved books. Henry's shy smile when he gave those to me flashed back through my memory and made me smile sleepily. I remembered him locking eyes with me as he said he looked forward to the ball. He was anticipating my presence at the gathering!

"For better or for worse." I whispered in the dark as my aunt's words came back to me from earlier. I smiled cheekily as my mind started dreaming up scenes of the ball next week. I was going to go to that ball, shine for Henry, and enjoy myself!

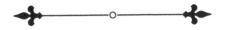

Chapter 3

W hat sound does the word cat start with?" I asked.

"Cuh, cuh, cuh." Emilee responded with a grin that showed off the gap in her mouth where she had lost her very first tooth.

"Good job!" I praised enthusiastically. "What about dog? What sound does the word dog start with?"

"Dog." She repeated. "Duh, duh, duh. My daddy just bought a new dog. He is brown and wiggly. My brothers love running with him."

"I am sure you will have fun playing with him this summer and teaching him tricks." I said. "I want you to sing the ABC song when you are at home doing your chores, alright? It will help you memorize all the letters."

"Okay. A, B, C, D, E, F, G ..... that is all I remember from earlier." She said with her starry gray eyes looking up into mine.

"H, I, J, K, L....." I repeated and continued to finish the song for her to remember. "I would like to hear you sing it for me tomorrow."

"Okay! I like your name, Miss Adelia because it starts with the very first letter of the alphabet." Emilee informed me.

I laughed. Emilee was such a sweet little girl and I enjoyed teaching her to read. Ms. Lynn hired me to work at her "Dame school", as most people call it, to teach her pupils how to read and paint. Ms. Lynn never had a formal education, so she could not teach young girls how to read and write very well. She had the brilliant revelation two years ago that if she could offer this service more families might enroll their daughters into her school. Her intuition was correct, and her house regularly swarms with eight to ten young girls five days out of the week. I was currently working with Emilee Clayton, who was five years old and extremely excited about being able to read complete chapter books in the future.

"Thank you, Emilee. That is a most unique and pleasing compliment." I told her.

"What is a compliment?" She asked.

"A compliment is when you praise someone for who they are or something that they have. You telling me that you like my name was a compliment." I explained.

Her eyes lit up as she contemplated what I had just told her. "Oh, I understand. So, when my daddy told me that he liked the way my mommy had braided my hair today, that was a compliment?" She asked for clarification.

"Yes, you are right, that is a good example." I spoke. "Why don't you come out into Ms. Lynn's garden where some of the other girls are drawing and painting. You can start working with the paints before you go home today."

Emilee started to jump up and down. "Yes, yes, yes! That sounds fun!"

I led her out of the library door and outside to where the easels and paint supplies were set up. "Hello, girls." I greeted the four other little ladies that were hard at work on artistic masterpieces.

"Hello!" They all responded perfectly in sync.

"Emilee is going to join you for a few minutes and play with the paints." I said as I helped her up onto a stool and tied a white apron over her red dress. "This will help paint to not splatter on your pretty dress."

Emilee was staring at the paints as if they were pieces of delicious candy. "I am going to use the red. Red is my favorite color." She told me.

I handed her a long brush and pointed over to Ms. Lynn's delicate red roses that were growing in a perfectly neat row, directly parallel to where the girls were set up. "Try to paint a rose with the red paint. You have a nice example right over there."

She nodded and her face scrunched up a bit as she started to concentrate. I left her in peace and walked by the easels to see my other pupils' work. They were coming along very nicely, and I could tell that they enjoyed working with artists' tools.

"Be a little bit smoother when drawing your lines, Sarah. I have found when working with graphite it is easier to correct your sketches if you begin drawing with light strokes." I admonished Sarah, a six-year-old girl who was very fond of sketching and painting.

"Yes, Miss Adelia." She said with a smile.

"I am going to go in and speak with Ms. Lynn. I will be back in a few minutes to help you put away the supplies." I communicated to the girls.

They nodded and I retreated into the house. I knew exactly where to find Ms. Lynn. She was usually in the living room instructing the young girls how to knit, sew, and crochet, but on a rare occasion, she would teach the girls how to bake something. I heard her voice in the kitchen and steered to the left to go to her.

"Adelia!" She called when she saw me step into the kitchen. "How many eggs do I put into my gingerbread cookies?" I mentally thought out her recipes that I have catalogued in my mind. As Ms. Lynn has gotten older I have found myself sometimes clarifying for her how much of what ingredient goes into which specific recipe.

"One egg, Ms. Lynn." I said cheerfully.

"Girls, we take the one egg and beat it into the mix very well. Next, we need to add in all of the dry ingredients." She instructed her avid listeners. "Here, you each take a turn mixing in the bowl."

She came over to speak to me. "I wanted to see if you could come over tomorrow evening to help me plant a few lavender bushes. I am planning to buy the plants in the morning at the market." She asked.

I cringed. She had mentioned that project to me a few days ago. The problem was tomorrow was Saturday, which I spend with my aunt and uncle typically, and the dance was in the evening!

"I cannot help you tomorrow evening, I am sorry." I replied sheepishly.

She looked at me suspiciously. "What plans do you have tomorrow evening? You look very mischievous."

"I was invited to the Ansley's ball. I am attending with my aunt and uncle." I said avoiding her poignant gaze.

"Ah! That is right, I had forgotten that event was tomorrow. The young women around Hastings have been buzzing about it most of the week." She commented. "But you are not truly interested in the social games between all the young people at dances are you?"

I blushed as I knew she was teasing me. "That is what I thought." She said with a knowing smile. "Enjoy yourself at the ball, and whichever young man you have set your sights on, I hope you get to dance with him."

I quickly looked up at her face, surprised at her comment. Ms. Lynn is approaching her late fifties and she has never married. It is sometimes hard to imagine that she had a romantic past, and her statement caught me off guard.

"Oh, surprised at what I said, yes? I was young once, just like you are now, and I remember the excitement of being in the presence of favorable young men. Alright, it is time for you and the girls to go home now." She said while shooing us out of the kitchen.

"Thank you, Ms. Lynn, and I can stay late on Monday to help with the lavender bushes!" I called as I walked out the door.

"Goodbye!" I heard her say.

I went back out to the garden and helped my little artists clean up the painting things. Emilee had painted a particularly good red rose for a girl of five who had never been exposed to painting or drawing before. She was most excited to go home to her family and show off her art to receive compliments.

I waved goodbye to my girls and began on the road home. The road was dusty as we had not had rain for a few days, and I could smell the pink and white wildflowers that were lining the fields on either side of my path.

After a few minutes of walking, I went past the Moore's house and saw my aunt coming out of the door. I waited for her, and she came over quickly.

"Hello!" I greeted her. "Did Emer have her baby yet?"

Leah shook her head. "No. The child is almost a week overdue. I am worried because I found out today that she is feeling weak, and she might have a fever. If she is ill when she goes into labor, her delivery will be harder."

I listened to her speak as we continued towards home. My aunt was well known in the community for her ability to work with herbs and remedies to help ailments. Emer Moore is a friend of my aunt's, and she wanted Aunt Leah present at the birth. Emer is five and thirty and heavily pregnant with her first child. She married at the age of thirty, and apparently had trouble getting pregnant for some time. The pregnancy has been awfully hard on her though. The Moore's moved from Ireland to England during the great famine. I could tell that Aunt Leah was worried about the outcome of the birth when it would eventually happen. I did not blame her. I know my mother died in childbirth delivering me and the thought of someday having to go through that process myself completely terrified me.

"Hopefully, the little one will come out soon." I chirped.

"Yes. Enough about that. How was your day?" She said with a cheerful smile.

I launched into the stories that I had about my students. "Emilee is such a darling. She is one of the first little girls that I have taught to really have a passion for learning to read. She is anticipating being able to read her favorite fairytales by herself that her mother reads to her. She reminds me of myself."

"You have always loved books. Even before you could read as a toddler, you would pull books off the low shelves and flip through the pages. I knew you needed to learn how to read as soon as possible." She explained. My aunt spent her precious time teaching me arithmetic and reading for several years when I was younger.

"If you had not been my personal teacher all those years ago, I would not be able to help the girls in Hastings." I reminded her.

"I am glad you enjoy your work. Goodness knows you could be doing plenty of other disagreeable things for an occupation." She told me.

Working for Ms. Lynn enables me to contribute towards the family expenses. I am ever so thankful I do not have to serve as a chambermaid or work at a factory.

"I am ready to get home." My aunt said. "A nice warm dinner and a cozy fire is just what I need right now."

"That does sound good. I was going to go over to Edith's house for a little bit. I will be back before supper at seven. We were going to discuss what we are planning to wear tomorrow night." I explained.

"That is exactly the kind of sacred gathering the two of you young ladies would come together for." My aunt said teasingly. "I can walk you to her house. Make sure that you start for home before dark falls." Aunt Leah advised me. I linked my arm through hers as we walked. My life seemed ever so blissful at this moment.

"Ow! That hurts, stop pulling." Edith exclaimed while batting my hands away from her hair. We were in front of her dressing mirror, and I was trying to help her arrange her hair in a fancy updo.

"Well, you need to comb through your hair again. There are too many knots to do anything suitable with it." I retorted as I released the locks that I was trying to pin-up.

She took ends of her blonde hair in a tight grip and began to forcefully tug her brush through the many tangled strands.

"Be careful! You are going to pull out more hair than what is in the knot." I warned her, somewhat appalled at how she was treating her tousled hair.

She ignored me while she tossed the brush on her dresser and dramatically collapsed onto her bed. "Tell me again what happened on the beach? I am ever so jealous that I was not there." She seethed. "Are you going to wear your blue dress or your pink dress tomorrow night?"

"I think I have decided on the blue because I have not worn it in a while, and I know you want to wear your pink dress."

"Are you sure? I do not want to hinder you if you would prefer to wear your pink dress." She asked.

"No! You must wear the pink one, Edith! The color is so flattering to your hair and skin tone. Besides, your pink gown is much fancier and more elegant than mine." I said wistfully as I fingered the silk fabric in her wardrobe. The soft pink dress had an off-the-shoulder neckline with dainty stitched roses that decorated the bodice. Edith's family had more annual income than my family did, so her parents could afford to buy her new gowns regularly.

Edith could sense my demeanor as she peered into my face. "You are going to look beautiful tomorrow night! It does not matter if you are the fanciest girl there, you will be stunning for Henry! Now tell me what he said to you last week!" She demanded. I started to tell her my story but was soon interrupted when Edith's two younger siblings burst into her room.

"Edith, do you know where my ball is?" Will, her younger brother of nine asked.

The Ideals of Adelia

"We need it because we want to play with it outside!" Dora, her younger sister of six informed her.

Edith looked quite frustrated at their question. "William! Dora!" She began. "How many times have I told you to not enter into my room without knocking?"

"A lot." Dora answered.

"That is right, but you never seem to listen. I do not know where your playthings are, and I want you out!" Edith said while shoving them both out of her room and slamming the door.

"Pests!" She muttered to me. "It is such a nuisance sometimes to have siblings so much younger than I am." Edith's parents were young when they got married. Her mother, Laura, had Edith when she was twenty, and then she had Dora and William later in life. I have noticed that Edith seems desperate to get married, most likely because she has her mother for an example as being wed at eighteen and then having her first child at Edith's age. I do believe my friend has a fear of becoming an old maid.

"They were just being curious." I defended her sibling's behavior. I was used to being around young children at Ms. Lynn's and I did not mind her brother and sister popping in.

"Well, you do not have to be with them all the time. I would have enjoyed an older sister." She grumbled.

That statement made me laugh. "I am the closest thing that you will get to having an older sister." I replied. Edith was born in March, and she just turned twenty, so I am about five months older than she is.

"Yes, besides if you were my sister and we were together constantly, we would probably both get on each other's nerves all the time." Edith decided.

"I agree with that." I giggled. Edith and I have had our spats over the years, but we have been friends for so long that I could never imagine not having her in my life. I delved into telling her my story from the beach as she listened attentively. After I finished, she looked deep in thought.

"Do you think Henry is trying to hint that he has feelings for you?" Edith pondered.

"Possibly. Hopefully!" I spoke. "Aunt Leah and I had a conversation that it is not very realistic to expect that a relationship will develop between us, because of our differing social statuses, but I have a deep feeling that something might happen."

"I think he likes you!" Edith said while her face crinkled up with joy. "Besides, in Pride and Prejudice, Mr. Darcy loved Lizzie even though she did not have wealth. It could happen to you!"

I smiled thinking about the story from one of my favorite books. "Well, I will not be genuinely content unless you are settled and happy with your true love. How do you think it is going with Oliver?"

Edith blushed. "Well, let's just say that I am hoping he will ask to dance with me tomorrow."

"I know. It feels as if our lives right now are a mixture of wishing and hoping for things that have not happened yet." I complained.

Edith nodded. "Someday we will be completely content Adelia."

I knew what she was saying, but her comment made me think. To what extent would it take until we both found true happiness?

Would securing a satisfactory match in matrimony fix everything in life?

The next evening, dressing for the ball was almost painstaking. I could not wait to arrive there and see Henry. While I was painfully being sinched into my corset, I realized that there was a chance he might have a girl there with him. There was no room for me to get my hopes up. I would just have to attend and assess the situation upon arrival.

I reached for my gown in my armoire. It consisted of sky-blue cotton fabric with capped puffed sleeves and was my best gown at that moment in time. A single blue rose rested on the direct center of the neckline. I put it on and started to fuss at the skirt. I knew most of the other women's dresses would be extravagant and full, but I was making do with what I had.

I sat down at my dressing mirror and started to arrange my hair. I heard a short knock. "Come in." I allowed.

Aunt Leah stuck her head around the door. "I came to check on you. That dress looks most flattering on you Adelia."

"Thank you for saying that." I responded with a lack of confidence.

She could tell that I was feeling discouraged. "Adelia you are a beautiful person because of who you are on the inside. Having money, or expensive clothes, or admiration from young men mean nothing if you have no personality and are not a kind person."

My aunt had been instilling this principle in me for many years as I was growing up. "I know. I believe you. My difficulty is that deep down I want the things that wealthy girls possess. I wish I had fine clothes and I long for Henry's attention! I know that if I had money his family would accept me, and he might truly consider me."

Aunt Leah had a pained expression on her face as she was processing what I was telling her. "Think about this Adelia. Would you want Henry to like you or love you because you were wealthy? Would you want to be in a relationship based on status and social class alone?"

I immediately knew what I would choose. "I would wish for him to sincerely love me for who I am, not solely for the status I possess."

She nodded. "Exactly. Greed and false pretenses would be the worst possible foundation of a courtship. What I would encourage you to do, is be exactly who you are meant to be, and if Mr. Ansley cannot see your true inner beauty and worth then he does not deserve you."

"Thank you, Aunt Leah. Besides, I cannot go to this ball moping."

"That is right! You must sparkle and be lively. That reminds me! I have something for you." She rushed out of the room and was back in a moment holding a small box. "This is for you. It was your mother's." She told me.

I opened the round silver scrolled case. Inside lay a beautifully simple pearl pendant on a silver chain. "This is lovely." I uttered.

"Your father gave it to your mother when she became his betrothed. I know I could have waited for when you are engaged to be married but I want you to have something special to wear tonight. This is your most important event of the year." I lifted my hair so she could clasp the jewelry around my neck. It looked beautiful and dainty laying against my collarbone and the pearl matched with my blue gown.

"I love this very much." I was looking down and holding the pendant in my fingers. "It makes me feel as if a small piece of her is with me."

She wistfully smiled and nodded her head in agreement. "What are you doing with your hair?"

"Edith told me I should wear my hair up and looped behind my ears. I was hoping to add a pretty clip or pins." I responded.

"Edith barely knows what she is talking about half of the time. Let me help you." She offered.

Half an hour later I was completely dressed and ready. The carriage ride over to the Ansley's property was splendid. The evening was warm with a note of summer sweetness. Dusk was approaching and I could see the glimmer of stars peeking out from the East where the night darkness was creeping in. Looking at the night sky always enthralls me. The sparkling dots captivate my attention and let me dream of unknown things for my future.

I sat back down from pushing my head out of the carriage window and fingered my curls. Aunt Leah helped me arrange a scooping updo with my natural curls framing my face. I shampooed my hair the night before so it would be fresh and clean. When I awoke to tolerably smooth curls, I knew it would not be a fight to arrange my hair for the ball. Aunt Leah was a great assistance for hairdressing, she used one of my thick paintbrushes to wrap a dampened curl around the base. This helped it form into ringlets that framed my face. I preferred this style as I sometimes worry that I have a large forehead.

After what seemed like an eternity, we arrived at the Ansley's driveway. Invisible butterflies fluttered through my chest as I stepped out of the carriage and saw the silhouettes of invited guests in the glowing windows. It seemed that it had taken months to get to this moment, but it had only been about two weeks. I was ready to go in and have the evening begin!

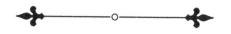

Chapter 4

Walking into the Ansley's house that night was thrilling. We stepped into the entryway and were greeted merrily by Mr. and Mrs. Ansley. Mrs. Ansley told us she was happy to see us and hoped we would enjoy the evening. We continued through the sea of people that had almost come to a standstill. It gave me a moment to fixate on the furnishings. Wood benches with lavish cream-colored cushions sat on either side of the staircase. Gilded mirrors hung on both sides of the massive fireplace mantle that rested against the cathedral height wall. I could see the young ladies glancing at their reflections, nervously checking to make sure everything about their appearance was perfect.

Candles were lit up and down the hallways, providing enough light to see, but the flames were flickering back and forth creating a perfect ambiance. We reached the staircase, and it was large and grand to behold. I felt weightless as I walked up it. A flurry of sights and sensations flashed through my senses as we walked towards the ballroom. I barely heard our names announced as I was most certainly overwhelmed with everything going on in the moment. A kaleidoscope of colors burst forth as I saw the girls adjusting their petticoats and skirts while young men fidgeted with their jackets and tousled hair. There was a distinctive hum throughout the large room as the people tried to carry out conversations over one another and musicians were fine-tuning their instruments. A barrage of smells assaulted my nose as I whiffed flowery perfumes and savory aromas of what was most likely our supper. I felt my stomach flip again, or was it a hunger pain? I cursed my sensitive stomach as I needed to focus on more important things other than food at the moment.

My aunt settled down with the other mothers and chaperones while my uncle made his way to the card room with the married men that were not at the ball for the purpose of making a romantic match. This left me by myself to mingle amongst the young people. I walked around searching for Edith and trying to keep an eye out for Henry. I finally spied her in the middle of a circle of three other girls. Edith has always been popular amongst the girls in Hastings. I trepidly walked over, making sure that my shoes did not purposefully clunk against the polished floor.

"Hello, Edith." I announced myself as I gave her a side hug.

"Adelia!" She said excitedly, her eyes lighting up. "Your dress looks marvelous! I knew it would be beautiful on you and is that a new necklace? Is not this so exciting! We were discussing how much fun these balls are."

I glanced over at the other young women standing near and instantly felt the weight of their captious eyes upon me. Agnes and Emma Langston were sisters a couple of years apart and they had a long-standing reputation of determining what an individual was worth to them based on what connections and wealth one's family possessed. The other young woman present was Bertha Winthrop who has the annoying habit of constantly sizing up what level of competition other young ladies are to herself. At this exact moment in time, she was staring me up and down, taking in the totality of my outfit and hair.

"It is new, thank you." I answered softly, hesitant to share details considering the current people present.

"That piece of jewelry is very quaint. Where did you get it?" Agnes asked.

"A friend gave it to me." I blurted out curtly. I did not like the false sweet tone she was using.

"Did your aunt pass it down to you?" Emma annoyingly butted in.

"A friend gave it to me." I repeated more forcefully. I wondered why I did not want to tell them it was passed down from my mother. It was not any of their business to ask me! Edith could see that I was uncomfortable and tried to change the subject.

"What are your favorite colors for dresses?" Edith asked all of us, continuing with her bubbly voice. "I particularly like this cornflower blue on Adelia."

"Yes that dress, it is.....darling on you." Bertha seemed to be searching for just the right word to not only describe my gown but also to act as disinterested as possible. "Have I seen you wear it before? At a tea party maybe?"

These girls were being pernicious. They were attempting to make me feel inferior in any way possible. Ignoring Bertha entirely, I mustered all my confidence as I turned to Edith. "I am going to get a cup of punch."

I turned away and was met with a smiling Clara Ansley and Mrs. Rachel Ansley standing right in front of me.

"Hello, Adelia!" Clara greeted me.

"Hello, Clara. Mrs. Ansley." I said with curtsies.

"Miss Hadlee." Mrs. Ansley announced. "Your hair is exceptionally pretty tonight. Your locks are naturally curly?"

I was equal parts shocked and honored that Henry's mother had complimented me and that she had said it in front of the petty young ladies that had tried their best to make me feel so small.

"Yes, these are my natural curls." I responded still in disbelief.

"I mentioned at a meal one night to my family how I have never met someone with such naturally beautiful long curls before. It is incredibly unique." Mrs. Ansley continued.

Mrs. Ansley was talking about my hair in front of her son Henry at her dining table, a detail that made me feel both baffled and joyous. I snuck a glance over at the other young ladies. Edith was smiling with happiness while the other girls looked as if they were about to implode with jealousy.

"Thank you. I inherited it from my aunt's family." I said shyly.

"Now that Clara has found her friends, I am going to check on a few of my other guests. Adelia, we can visit more later." Mrs. Ansley left and sauntered past the other girls.

"Hello, girls." She chirped and continued on her way.

"Hello, Mrs. Ansley!" Agnes and Emma cooed after her in their sickeningly sweet voices. While Mrs. Ansley was still within earshot, the girls pounced on Clara all at once like cats stalking a ball of yarn.

"Clara you look so beautiful tonight!" Emma exclaimed as she began to pet the ribbons on Clara's dress.

"You live in such a magnificent house, Clara." Agnes cooed.

"Your dress is lovely. What fabric is this?" Bertha purred.

Edith and I exchanged quiet glances at their ridiculous behavior. Clara looked confused and dazed as they swarmed about her, continually buzzing like honeybees. She said hello and then turned to me and grabbed my arm.

"Did you say you wanted to get something to drink?" She asked with pleading eyes.

"Yes." I said, staggered at her reaction to the other girl's behavior. We started walking over to a few separate tables. "Are you alright?" I questioned.

"I am fine, although I do not appreciate the way those girls behave around me. They act extremely interested in me, but I have a strange suspicion they are far more interested in my brothers than myself." She said with a perfected side-eye and an arched brow.

I was impressed that Clara had come to that conclusion on her own. She may act immature at times, but I underestimated her. "Good for you for making that connection." I praised.

She smiled sheepishly. "Enough of that. Let us go get a drink. The punch has ice cream in it!"

"It is all so fancy." I told her.

"Isn't it wonderful?" She asked rhetorically. As she said that I realized that she had probably never been without luxury all her life.

After reaching the refreshments table, I noticed Clara had led me straight to her brothers Henry and Oliver. They were standing in front of us, each holding two cups of punch.

"I see two pretty ladies who might be in need of a drink?" Oliver said while winking at his sister.

"Oh, Oliver!" Clara said and took a cup. Henry smiled at me, flashing his dimples, and offered me a dainty punch glass filled with the most colorful liquid I had ever laid eyes on. He was wearing a navy long coat and a cream necktie that made him appear absolutely dashing. I thought it fascinating that we had both chosen to wear blue hues in our outfits on the same evening.

"Hello. Thank you, Mr. Ansley." I said timidly.

"You are welcome, Miss Hadlee. How are you tonight?" Henry asked. His dark brown eyes were glistening orbs as he exchanged pleasantries with me. I had to take a deep breath, looking away momentary, to regain my composure.

"I am doing well. I am extremely excited to be here. Everything looks exquisite." I said and glanced around the ballroom again. Two chandeliers hung from the ornate ceiling and were dripping with dozens of candles. The light was darting back and forth across the room, its movement reminded me of tiny fairies flying around the room, sprinkling romantic wishing dust on all of the young couples.

"Mother did a great job arranging all of the details." Henry agreed. "And it seems that my siblings are having a good time." We both glanced over at Oliver and Clara to see Oliver teasing her about something that had to do with the ribbon in her hair. She was giggling and trying to poke back at him. Henry and I met eyes and started laughing at their immature antics. At that moment, the gaggle of snitty ladies walked by and I could feel the proverbial heat of their prolonged, gaping stares at the back of my head. I could not help but wonder if Henry had observed their ill-mannered behavior this evening.

"What is so funny?" Edith popped up out of nowhere.

I saw Oliver snap to attention out of the corner of my eye when he noticed that Edith had come over.

"Nothing important." Henry answered, minimizing the humor that had come from his sibling's behavior.

"Mr. Ansley. Clara." Edith acknowledged Henry and Clara. She turned to Oliver. "Mr. Oliver."

"Miss Edith." Oliver let Edith take his arm and led her over a few feet away, to a couple of other tables that were stacked with plates of scrumptious tarts and tiny cakes for refreshments. We could hear Edith giggling and Oliver talking in low tones into her ear. Clara looked at Oliver with her eyes wide as if she were scandalized by their behavior.

"Oliver is in love!" Clara tantalizingly announced to us. She apparently found her brother's romantic endeavors an open topic to discuss sensationally with us.

Henry shook his head with a bemused expression. "Is everything a joke to you Clara?" He chastised with a hint of a smile. Clara knew he was not truly mad at her, and she annoyingly ignored her older brother's reproof.

"Most definitely." She answered in response to his question and then retreated to the other side of the room to tease Oliver some more.

What Clara said about Oliver being in love panged something in my chest. I wanted her to be saying that about Henry in regard to myself! I watched Oliver and Edith for a moment. They looked like opposites, her with her blonde hair and blue eyes and his head full of short chestnut waves, and the same deep brown eyes as Henry. Their heights were matched perfectly, Edith being a little bit shorter than Oliver so that she could look up into his face and meet his eyes but have him still be taller than herself. I have always thought Oliver's mouth was too small for his face though. I suppose Edith does not seem to notice or does not care. He is handsome enough, but I felt that Henry was exceptionally more attractive.

I turned back to Henry and saw that he was also observing his brother. "All teasing aside, my younger sister seems to be right. Oliver is quite enamored with your friend."

"Clara better be careful. When it comes to be her turn for courting, she will get what she gives out to her siblings now in terms of goading about romance." I told him.

Henry chuckled and seemed to be processing this new revelation as he watched me. "Clara likes you. It has been nice to see her gain a friendship with such a sincere young lady as yourself."

Henry's comment made me ponder that maybe he did realize some of the other girls attending the ball this evening were not genuine in their interactions. I perked up at him calling me sincere. It seemed that I was getting closer to gaining real ground with Henry.

"Thank you, Mr. Ansley."

"You can call me Henry, Miss Adelia. I hope we are at a point in our familiarity that we can call each other by our first names." He offered.

"I would like that very much." I responded nervously, biting my lower lip. He made me feel so fluttery!

Henry set his cup down and launched into a new question. "I have heard you are especially fond of dancing Miss Adelia. Is this true?"

"Whoever would have told you that?" I asked with pretend shock.

"I have my sources." His eyes looked sly as he appeared secretive. The musicians were poised, and I could see couples lining up. It felt like I had been lost in conversation with Henry much longer than a couple of minutes.

"It is true. I enjoy dancing very much." I confirmed.

"In that case, would you like to dance the first dance with me?" Henry held out the golden invitation that I had been aspiring for. I almost felt lightheaded when I heard him say those words. I was stuck staring at him and his winning smile in a shocked daze.

"Oh no. No response is usually not a good sign." Henry said as an aside with a fake solemn expression as if he was upset at the prospect of not dancing with me.

I laughed and blushed simultaneously. "No, it is not that at all! Nothing would please me more than to dance with you, Henry."

He took my gloved hand with his strong but gentle grip and led me to the beginning line of the arranged couples. His hands were slender, but with strong, well-formed fingers and his palms were in the range of perfectly broad, not wide. The music started to swell up and my ears recognized that it was a romantic slow waltz that I would be dancing with him. I looked around at the other couples. I saw Edith and Oliver a few couples down and she caught my eye with an excited, "I cannot believe this is happening" look. I discreetly grinned back and turned to face Henry. We mutually reached for each other's hand while his right hand settled on my back under my left arm. We started to circle and sway as the music went into a crescendo.

"You dance exceedingly well. How did you learn?" He curiously asked.

"My aunt taught me." I replied as he spun me out and turned me back.

"Do not be unnecessarily humble, Adelia. I believe you are as much of a natural at dancing as you are at painting."

Henry had remembered and purposefully mentioned my art skills. It made my head continue to spin dizzily. I looked into his dark eyes as he gave me another perfect smile. I suddenly saw Bertha staring at me viciously from the dancing floor sidelines. Apparently, no young man had asked her to dance yet, and she seemed infuriated at the sight of me dancing with one of the most eligible bachelors in the room. I stumbled out of the turn I was trying to execute, but Henry smoothly steadied me with his hands and kept us dancing without the slightest of a missed step.

"Are you alright?" His face creased with concern.

"Yes." I muttered.

"What has you so distracted Miss Adelia?" Henry asked me kindly as we passed each other in a turn.

"I was noticing the number of young ladies watching me dance with you." I responded hesitantly. "It makes me feel uneasy."

He gave a lighthearted laugh at my remark. "Ah yes, that would be because you are one of the few girls, other than my sister, that I will probably choose to dance with tonight. Please do not let their disappointment make you feel unsettled."

"I will try. So, a dance with you is hard to come by then? A rare experience indeed." I said lightly.

"Yes, exceptionally rare. Only a special young lady would entice me to ask her for a dance."

I blushed and then continued on the current topic. "I get frustrated when other people's judgmental behavior affects my inner emotion."

His eyebrows furrowed. "Whatever do you mean?"

"Again, I challenge you to look around at all the prying eyes that are watching us dance. " I commanded in a whisper.

He discreetly looked around the spacious room as I spun out again and responded once we were back to stepping back and forth. "People are always going to be watching." He told me matter-of-factly.

"I suppose that is one of my weaknesses then." I sighed. "Worrying about what others are scrutinizing and deciding about me."

"I have not really considered that subject before. I cannot determine if that is something I should worry about now or ever." He teased lightly.

"You have true confidence. A desirable quality."

"I do have one weakness though." Henry announced to me. The lead violin's notes were starting to die down and our steps were slowing.

I was intrigued. "What would that be?"

"The jade green eyes of one's dancing partner." He stated, deeply looking into my viridescent eyes as we faced each other. At that moment, the dance we had shared came to an end. I was speechless, and I felt the heat flush straight into my cheeks. It certainly was warm in the ballroom this evening.

"Miss Hadlee." He bowed.

"Mr. Ansley." I curtsied. I could not believe what my ears had heard him say. The couples dispersed and a few other young men surrounded Henry and started talking in a boisterous manner. He looked back at me one last time and then moved forward with his friends. I silently slid back into the sidelines. My dance with Henry had ended but he had filled my hopeful heart to its brim.

I surveyed the room once more to see what the current activities were. The young girls were walking the floor, making eyes at the men, increasingly desperate for a partner for the second dance. Oliver and Edith were still chatting, and I had no doubt that they were going to dance again next. I did not expect Henry to ask me again, but I was thoroughly happy that he had danced the first dance with me. Indeed, I believe I had not stopped smiling since we had parted ways.

I saw Aunt Leah sitting on a purple chaise deep in conversation with Mrs. Ansley. I wondered what they were talking about and walked over.

"She has always shown a true amount of maturity for her age. It takes a real level of strength for a young person in that situation." I heard my aunt say as I approached. She smiled when she caught sight of me, and Mrs. Ansley beckoned me over with a wave. I sat down next to Aunt Leah, and she ruffled my curls.

"Hello, Adelia. How are you getting along?" Aunt Leah inquired happily. Even though she was not at the dance for courtship purposes, the liveliness and romanticism of the event put a youthful glow on her cheeks.

My smile beamed as I was at the brink of exploding with euphoria from my dance with Henry, but I had to keep my emotions in check with his mother observing me. "I am well." I modestly answered.

"We were speaking of you a few moments ago." Aunt Leah said mischievously.

"What about me?" I said hesitantly.

"Leah tells me you teach young girls how to read and write. Do you enjoy your occupation?" Mrs. Ansley asked.

"I do enjoy it tremendously. All of my pupils are sweet in temperament and possess a desire to learn."

"It is charitable that you use your education to help the children." Mrs. Ansley praised. "I have always thought it is important for children of all social classes to be literate."

"Especially young girls. More often than not, underprivileged young women who are Adelia's age can barely write their own name." Aunt Leah said with a sorrowful effect.

Rachel nodded but the emotion on her face reflected that she was going to add to my aunt's comment. "I agree with you Leah, but I sometimes wonder when it will be enough. Now society is pushing for women to have the same level of university education as men. There is nothing wrong with literate women, but they should be focused on their feminine role in society and their household. Girls do not need male nonsense filling up their minds."

My aunt and I took this information in quietly. Obviously, Mrs. Ansley had formed her firm opinion on this matter. I cleared my throat. "Well, I am teaching these young girls painting techniques. That is an accomplished skill."

She drew herself out of her hardened ideals. "Oh yes, that's right. Clara mentioned you have a skill for painting. Speaking of her, she certainly is getting her share of dancing in!" The music had started up for the second dance and I glanced around with interest, looking to see who Clara was dancing with and curious to know if Henry had chosen a second dance partner. I let out a sigh of relief I did not realize I was holding when I saw Henry and Clara dancing together. I smiled to myself while Mrs. Ansley continued discussing different topics with my aunt that were irrelevant to me. I grew bored. It was much more mesmerizing to observe the couples and process my previous interaction with Henry. My eyes gravitated towards watching him with a constant discreetness. I could not help it, and sometimes I did not even realize I was doing it! I hoped his mother would not notice, as she seemed preoccupied with talking.

"Adelia? How long have you been friends with Edith?" Mrs. Ansley's voice cut through my almost daydreams and my brain had to process what I had heard her say.

"I have known her since we were little girls. She has been my closest friend since I can remember." I told her, purposefully choosing words that would put Edith in a good light.

"Edith is a very pleasant young lady." My aunt remarked.

Mrs. Ansley was watching Edith and her son dance with interest. "Clara has told me she gets along so well with you and Edith, Adelia." She said with a motherly smile. I felt warmth in my chest when she praised me. She continued speaking about her son. "It is fairly noticeable what Oliver's intentions are. It seems that he will be the first of my sons to make a match." At those words, I felt that unignorable twinge of envy. I yearned for her oldest son to be making a match with me! As I continued swirling through the thoughts and emotions in my mind, I barely noticed that Mrs. Ansley had left and that my aunt and I were alone monotonously watching the current dance finish.

"Henry danced with you!" Aunt Leah suddenly burst out with a hushed whisper.

I turned to her with a look of delight. "I know! I can barely believe it. And I think he was at ease with me throughout it." I sighed.

My aunt was laughing and watching me. "This makes you happy, yes?"

"Immensely happy."

"Alright, we will talk later. You should go enjoy yourself while you are here. Try to dance again with someone else. A certain amount of competition might help prod Henry along even more." She encouraged me.

"I agree." My lips were parched from dancing and talking. "I need something to drink before I dance again. Can I get you something?"

"I am fine." She nodded me off. I sauntered over to the refreshment table and chose a glass of bright lemonade. It proved to be refreshing and tart. I was about to go mingle through the groups of people when I paused as I heard my name across the partition that stood between the drink and dessert tables. I strained to hear over the giggles of young girls and loud voices of men in the background.

"Did you see Adelia dancing with Henry Ansley?" I heard Emma say with a degree of vexation. "The nerve of that girl! She is younger than us by three years, so one would reason that we should have the pick of the suitors, not her."

"Not to mention our dowries are much larger than that little pest's will ever be." Agnes added.

"It is frustrating that he danced the first dance with her. That might indicate something. He stood up with his sister after that, but he has not danced since. What if he actually does like Adelia?"

"Do not worry Emma, no respectable man such as Mr. Henry Ansley would be genuinely interested in marrying a poor, insignificant orphan like Adelia Hadlee." Agnes concluded.

They both snickered and walked away, leaving me with the bitter taste of lemons on my palate. They acted as if I had been the initiator of the dance, but Henry had obviously approached me. Their vile words cut me to the core, but I had an invisible shield up that had been reinforced from years of their callous behavior. A look of amusement descended upon my face as I realized how truly upsetting it had been for those self-absorbed girls that Henry had shown himself attentive to me. I had never felt more satisfied with the timely outcome of any one specific event in my entire life. I set my glass down and turned on my heels to continue with my night. I almost ran right into Arthur Barlow, who was waiting to speak with me.

"Miss Hadlee. How are you?"

"I am well Mr. Barlow." Arthur was the grandson of Mr. and Mrs. Barlow, and we were all close family friends. He asked me to dance, and I accepted. I was hoping that Henry was watching from wherever he had positioned himself.

After I danced with Arthur, it was time for the meal, which worked out well since the Barlow's were assigned to the same table as us. I sat between my aunt and Arthur. As I suspected, Oliver escorted Edith to his table. She was sitting next to her beau and on her other side was her future sister-in-law Clara. Interestingly, Henry had not taken any young woman to dinner with him. He sat next to his mother and his sister. I had known better than to expect a seat next to him at the Ansley's table. I was extremely excited for Edith, however. She and Oliver had been inseparable most of the night.

The meal was scrumptious and unbelievably detailed. The first course was a brothy cream soup with vegetables and a type of mild white fish. The main dish had a plate full of savory lamb roast with a combination of wild herbs and spices. Finally, the waiters served everyone a heaping plate with what looked like shiny dark green leaves and other vegetables with cheese sprinkled throughout. I stared at it in awe, wondering what it was.

My aunt was watching me curiously and explained in a low voice, "It is a salad Adelia, made with lettuce. Taste it."

I stabbed the greens with my fork and put a bite into my mouth. The lettuce was crunchy and tasted as if it was filled with water. The shiny layer on the lettuce leaves was a liquid dressing that tasted sweet and savory at the same time. Hints of garlic, onion, and cheese flavors danced on my tongue. I finished my food with gusto. It was so difficult to keep my manners and act like a lady while wanting to eat each bite with vigor. My favorite had most certainly been the salad. I sat back as others were finishing their food and conversation was escalating around the table. As usual, the men were discussing current issues that were taking place in the world.

"The Irish were occupying all the available jobs here when they immigrated during the potato blight." Barked Mr. Brown, a middle-aged bachelor who was seated with us.

"And John Mitchel's journal that he published in 1848 encouraged the Irishman to revolt against the British soldiers." Mr. Barlow stated.

"He deserved his arrest for treason." Mrs. Barlow interjected with a hurt look. Their son had been a soldier and was killed in a most violent event between Irishmen and the soldiers a few years ago. Arthur's mother then died a few months later from scarlet fever, leaving him an orphan, living with his grandparents.

"There are still Irish immigrating today?" Arthur asked.

"Yes some, but the numbers have dwindled now that Ireland is in a better economic state." Uncle Richard clarified.

"Thank goodness for that." Mrs. Barlow concluded. "We do not need their men and children over here taking up land, jobs, and bringing diseases."

My inner conscience was pricking me at the way they were describing the Irish immigrants. "The Irish are fellow human beings, the same as us. Why treat them with contempt?" I could not hold my tongue.

The older adults turned to me in surprise. "They are different than us. All they brought with them was savagery and unrest." Mr. Barlow lamented.

"Are the British incapable of showing compassion?" I tried to reason. "Their families and children were starving, and yet the soldiers were ruthless and showed no mercy." Out of the corner of my eye, I could see both my aunt and uncle watching me with growing interest.

"My, you speak your mind freely." Mr. Brown commented.

"These subjects are not fit for a young woman of your age to be dwelling on Adelia!" Mrs. Barlow chastised with a critical frown.

I flushed and cast my eyes to my plate. I did not want to be embarrassed for speaking what I thought to be the truth, but her rebuke made me feel gauche.

"In general, these topics should not be discussed at a dinner party." My uncle concluded.

Arthur leaned over. "You have compassion, which is an important value for a young woman."

I knew he was trying to lessen the sting of being reprimanded in front of everyone at the table, but I still felt uncomfortable. I kept to myself and wondered what Henry was contemplating over at his table. Did he feel the delight of these events the entire evening, or did his morale drop halfway through the night, making it difficult to keep the enthusiasm? My exuberance had been sapped and the food settling on my stomach made me feel full and sleepy. The meal had concluded, and all of the guests were now getting up and shuffling back into their respective rooms of interest. Ladies and young men went back to the ball room for dancing, and older men and women into another room for card games. I danced a few more sets with various men that I have been familiar with through the years, and then I sat back down to rest. It was approaching half past midnight, and I was feeling fatigued. I found a spot next to Edith, who was also taking a break.

"How have you been?" I asked her. I did not really need a verbal answer from her, as her face said it all. Her eyes were sparkling, and a beaming smile was painted across her lips.

"Terrific!" She grasped my hands and squeezed them excitedly. "Oliver danced the first two dances with me. I do not think I have to wonder anymore about what our relationship status is!"

I shook my head in agreement. "He took you to supper, and both his mother and Henry acknowledged that you two are getting close."

"So, you have been talking to Henry? I saw you dancing with him, and I was overjoyed. What did he say to you while dancing?"

I told her about our exchange. She crinkled her nose in surprise and giggled. "He does like you! Did you say anything back to him?"

"No, I was too shocked to think of anything witty to say in response."

"Adelia, you have to encourage him a little bit." She instructed me. "Flirt and laugh when he is near you. I am sure he will find it playful. What did his mother say about me?"

"She was asking how long you and I have been friends; I think she wants information on your character. I put in a good word for you."

"Well, I should hope it was the truth." She scoffed in a teasing tone.

"Of course!" I responded. We were still giggling and chatting when I heard someone's voice behind me.

"Is this seat taken?" I turned around at the sound of Henry's modulated voice. His voice warm and pleasing in tone.

"No." I said and gestured for him to sit down. He relaxed his posture against the bench alongside me and I smiled.

"How are you?" He wondered.

"I am a little bit tired. I feel like being at social events saps your energy somewhat." I explained.

He nodded. "There are crowds of people at these parties. It is exhausting trying to navigate through circles of people that I do not even know yet."

"That is right! You have only been here for a few months. You likely do not know half of the people who are coming up to speak with you." I reasoned.

He agreed and continued. "Yes, and it is especially strange when I have an adult who is a relative or a friend of my parents who comes up to me and informs me that they remember me when I was a child."

"Yes, they remember you, but you definitely do not remember who they are." I acknowledged, knowing that feeling.

"Exactly!" We were both laughing now. "What are you supposed to say to that?"

Edith popped her head over into our proximity. "Henry, what is your middle name? Clara and I were talking about the importance of middle names at supper, and she said I should ask what your and Oliver's middle names are."

Henry slightly smiled. "Shouldn't you ask Oliver himself what his middle name is?"

She rolled her eyes. "Fine! I guess I will just have to go talk to him again." Edith smiled and turned back to one of her friends with whom she was talking to, leaving me to continue my conversation with Henry.

"Now I want to know what your middle name is. Will you tell me?" I inquired.

"Well, I am afraid that my names are not as exciting as others might be." Henry explained while growing shy. He seemed to act extremely modest when he spoke about himself. "My mother chose the name Henry as she had favored that name for years. My middle name is Matthew, after my father. I am their eldest son." He turned the question to me with a roguish smile. "What is your middle name?"

Sharing these personal details with each other made me feel close to him. "My mother's name was Jolee, and my middle name is her namesake. It seems that we share having the namesakes of our parents in common."

"It seems that we do." He answered while looking into my eyes again. The intensity of his stare made me light-headed, and I began to wonder if he did hold some regard for me. It was almost as if he was studying me, and I desperately wished to know what he was thinking. I bit my lip as I looked away and noticed my aunt and uncle standing nearby, talking to another set of parents. I saw my aunt glance at me and smile. It was extremely late, and I knew that they were both getting ready to go home. I looked back to Henry who had been addressed by another young man. They were both eagerly talking, and I then saw my aunt and uncle coming over to where I was. I said goodbye to Edith and got up to walk over to my family. I was disappointed that Henry had not stopped to say goodnight to me, but I realized it would have been rude to interrupt his conversation.

"Are you ready to go?" Aunt Leah asked in her loving way.

"Yes." I responded tiredly. As we passed by Henry again on our way to find his parents so we could bid our goodbyes, I saw him observing me once more. I looked back and he smiled at me in his reserved, but stately way. I matched his gaze and gently waved goodbye. A reverential grin occupied my face the entire carriage ride home. I could not wait to go to sleep, as I was assuredly hopeful Henry would accompany me once more in my dreams.

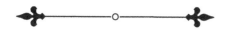

Chapter 5

"Adelia." My mind was drifting through a perpetual dream state when my aunt's voice roused me. About a week had passed since the ball when this particular interruption in my sleep occurred. I moaned, trying to turn over in an attempt to ignore her and return to my lovely dreams.

"Adelia, you must get up." My aunt shook my shoulder with a sense of urgency. "Emer Moore went into labor a few hours ago, I am going to need your help. She is still fighting some sort of sinus and chest ailment."

I sighed and stiffly sat up as my warm sheets twisted and grabbed at my legs, trying to lure me to stay in their grasp. "Give me a few minutes." I croaked and climbed out of my nest to get dressed. She left and I lit a candle to illuminate my room. My face recoiled as the sharp amber light hit my puffy green eyes and temporarily blinded me for a couple of seconds. As my eyes adjusted, I traipsed over to my armoire and pulled out a simple cotton gown that was perfectly adequate for an excursion in the wee hours of the morning. I clamped my hair with a large clip, crammed my stockinged feet into my low walking boots, wrapped a light crocheted shawl around my shoulders, and met Aunt Leah at the front door. She was holding a lantern and her shoulder apothecary bag. My uncle was standing next to her waiting with his own lantern.

"I am going to walk you ladies over to the Moore's. I assume you will not be back until later in the morning?" Uncle Richard spoke up.

I had grown accustomed to his instinct to protect us as women, and it made me feel secure.

Aunt Leah shook her head in confirmation, and we hastily ushered ourselves out the door. Three pairs of feet crunched and clomped on the dirt gravel road as we swiftly traveled to Emer's house. I was thankful that it was not the middle of winter, as the thin air felt crisp and biting even though we were a month away from the summer solstice. The bright glow of the full moon shone down across the dark expanse, illuminating a pathway to the Moore's house. A high-pitched howl rose in the eerie silence, and I halted in place, my eyes widening in alarm.

My uncle heard me gasp. "It is a coyote Adelia, you are fine." I saw his amused expression in the lantern light. My family knows that I tend to get excitable when it comes to wild animals and frightening occurrences. I pulled my shawl closer to my chest and pushed on. The Moore's small farm home was about a mile up the road and it came into view soon enough. The house was alight with candles and lanterns shining through the glass windows. My aunt marched up to the front door and I heard her thumping knock resound on the solid walnut door worn from decades of use.

I turned back to my uncle. "Are you going to be alright walking back by yourself?"

He smiled at my concern. "Yes, I will be fine. I will ask Alice to hold your breakfast until you are home. Now go help your aunt." He commanded as the Moore's door opened and Aunt Leah slipped inside. I followed her as we walked past Emer's husband, who had answered the door.

"Hello, John." My aunt said dismissively when Emer's husband grunted at us. Aunt Leah rushed to the bedroom where Emer was located. My brow furrowed at my aunt's tone. John and Emer have been in our community for a couple of years, but I did not know them very well. I did not have time to think about what their exchange meant as I heard deep breaths and cries of pain followed by coughing fits in the next room. I followed in behind my aunt, just in time to witness Leah rubbing Emer's back as she drew in tight, ragged breaths that rattled on their way out.

"How are you doing Emer?" Aunt Leah asked with a calm tone. She had the amazing ability to maintain a tranquil demeanor when tending to those who are in great amounts of pain or are ill and in despair.

Emer breathed in sharply, very sharply, it was almost as if she was sucking in all her air. The air came back out as a long string of hacking coughs. "This is the worst pain I have been in." She barely whispered through clenched teeth. She continued to cough and take wheezing breaths. "Of course, it does not help that I can barely breathe!"

"Has a Doctor seen you since you've been ill?" Leah asked while sitting her apothecary bag down on the edge of the bed. Emer shook her head no. "Is the midwife coming?" My aunt asked, her voice getting tight.

"We cannot afford a blasted Doctor." John spat from the corner of the room. I turned in surprise as I had not heard him come in. His untucked shirt and dirt-stained pants made for a disheveled appearance and the smell of liquor arose off his breath.

My aunt ignored his comment and turned to me. "I need you to make some hot tea water. We are going to need much more hot water soon, but right now I need you to prepare some mint tea for Emer."

I nodded and went over to my aunt's bag to root around for the mint tea leaves.

"We are going to get you comfortable, Emer." I heard Aunt Leah reassuring her. "I have some experience in childbirth, and we mostly need to let your body take over. Let us try to soothe that cough for now."

I had never made a cup of tea so quickly in my life. I knew that the mint would help relieve her aching throat from the urge of coughing, and I had been instructed to add lemon balm for a light sedative. When I came back with the drink, Emer was lying down in a fresh nightgown and my aunt had a cool cloth on her forehead. As Emer drank the tea, Aunt Leah applied a therapeutic lavender compress to her upper chest in hopes of alleviating congestion. My aunt dutifully tended to her and got her situated, propping her up with plenty of pillows. After a good amount of time, Emer's breathing improved, and Aunt Leah was able to assist her in using her breaths to go along with the pain. When my aunt came over to get something else from her satchel, I sprung at her with essential questions.

"Is she going to be fine? Do we know what we are doing? How much longer?" I asked anxiously.

"Stay calm Adelia. The most important thing about taking care of a person in distress is to stay levelheaded and keep your focus on the patient." I nodded in agreement and took a deep breath. "Her pain is going to increase for a short time and then she will deliver. You have to help me when the baby comes." I swallowed hard and hazily agreed. I was nervous, but I knew both Aunt Leah and Emer needed me, and I was determined to stay strong.

An hour later we were witness to the horrendous threshold of pain that my aunt had described. Emer was crying out and she had my hand in a death grip as she pushed. My aunt was at the foot of the bed preparing for the baby to make his or her entrance. Through this entire experience, Emer's husband had been silently watching or broodily pacing in the hallway outside the open bedroom.

"Keep pushing Emer. A couple of big pushes and then we are there. Come on now. Give it everything that you have to give." My aunt admonished.

Emer's sweaty face scrunched up as she mustered her remaining energy into one last massive push. A tiny pink, wet, and wrinkly human being slipped out into my aunt's hands and began to wail. Emer seemed to relax and dropped my hand from her grasp.

"It is a baby girl!" Aunt Leah cried out. The tiny being was thrashing about and kicking in my aunt's hands. She placed her on Emer's chest and Emer started cooing and talking to her baby. While we were preparing for the after birth, and the baby was learning how to suckle for food, Emer suddenly cried out in pain once again.

"What is it?" I asked, studying her face in alarm.

"It hurts really bad again." She puffed out and continued to breathe sharply.

"Delivering the placenta should not be causing this amount of pain." My aunt announced. Concern for Emer's condition increased as I heard her moan with pain. This was reminding me of the fact that my own mother had died giving birth to me. I grabbed the small child as Emer started contracting and pushing again. "I will take the baby." I informed them as my aunt nodded at me and focused on helping Emer. I took a fluffy towel and brought the tiny baby girl into the kitchen to find a wash basin. I encountered John Moore slouched in a chair at the table. I was hoping to ignore him, but he decided to accost me.

"What is she doing in there?" He first inquired and then saw the bundle in my arms. "Is that the baby?"

"Yes, you have a baby girl." I answered as I filled the clean basin with tepid water. His face darkened when he heard the sex of his new child.

"How is a useless girl going to help me with the farm?" He rhetorically asked and pounded the table with his fist. Anger at his words bubbled forth in my chest, replacing the chronic worry that had filled it earlier. I could not hold my tongue.

"As you sit here wallowing in disdain for the child that you had a part in bringing into this world, your wife is suffering in the other room." I turned my back on the disagreeable man as he contemplated my words.

"Emer wanted a child, not me!" He announced and stalked out into the other room. I was glad that he left as it gave me and the baby peace and quiet. I started to wash her, as she fussed and kicked at the stimulus.

"I know, I know. You are fine. I am almost done." I told her. She had a full head of dark hair and squishy cheeks. Her cries were not more than little meows, and I had decided that she was entirely precious. I wrapped a cloth around her waist and swaddled her in a teensy soft dressing gown and blanket that I had found in a bureau nearby. She began drifting asleep as I softly held her in my arms. I suddenly heard more wailing coming from the bedroom and I hurried back in, holding the little girl. My aunt was holding a second baby.

"She has delivered twin girls!" My aunt told me while smiling immensely. I breathed a sigh of relief as I realized Emer was going to be fine. I brought over the first child as my aunt wrapped up the second.

"Congratulations Emer." I whispered as I handed over her first daughter and stepped back.

"I am exhausted." Emer whispered and closed her eyes as she rested her head on the pillow.

"I think you have earned the right to be tired." I said with a smile.

She smiled and opened her eyes. "Thank you so much, Leah and Adelia."

"They are beautiful Emer." My aunt praised as she brought back the second baby from washing and dressing her.

"They are two extra mouths to feed." John spat. The tingling anger I felt earlier returned, and his comment made me seethe. Aunt Leah and I locked eyes and I could sense her frustration growing with the ignorant man.

"Well John, it seems you should have thought of that before you committed to having children with your wife. In the meantime, you had better get used to being a father to your daughters." She said forcibly while thrusting one of the babies into his arms. He quickly grabbed her and was surprisingly attentive to the baby's squirming while he intently watched his child. Emer seemed relieved that her husband's attitude and my aunt's reaction had not escalated into a high temper flare-up.

Soon enough the two babies had entered the newborn state of wanting to sleep and Emer herself seemed so near exhaustion that she could barely talk to us and keep her eyelids open as we got ready to leave. My aunt sweetly, yet sternly, admonished John to keep a strict watch on Emer and help her in any way possible with the new babies. Aunt Leah promised her friend that she would come over and check on the new family in two days' time.

The two of us walked home in the brisk early morning air. Summer was calling through the sunshine that lit up the path, but the coastal breeze blew into our faces, dashing my hopes of warm weather. I was guessing it was about seven o'clock on the hour or so.

"Are you very tired?" My aunt asked after I had yawned in the middle of a sentence.

I was extraordinarily tired from being pulled out of my bed so early and then experiencing Emer giving birth. It also did not help that the last few nights after the ball, I had been reliving memories that were full of Henry in my mind. I would feel excitably restless when I retired to sleep, pondering his actions and imagining future conversations. When I did finally get to sleep, he smoothly danced through my dreams, making me curse the sunrise, for I knew my bliss was only momentary.

"Yes, I am tired. I am yearning to slip back into my cozy bed to catch up on lost sleep." I sighed.

"Well, we are almost back to Cliffside." She said as we passed the familiar bend in the path that signaled we were three minutes away. "You have not been sleeping well? Could this be a symptom of being in a preoccupied state when it comes to affairs of the heart my sweet girl?" She gave me a teasing glance as she watched me look away. I honestly believe my aunt is a mind reader, as she can always pinpoint my emotions and knows my inner motivations so well.

"Maybe I am in love." I responded quietly.

"As long as you are not in love with a man like John Moore." Her words were tainted with a slight growl of resentment.

"Oh, he is almost despicable!" I eagerly shared my feelings. "How can someone be so unappreciative and disrespectful to their spouse?"

"It is more common than not." Aunt Leah told me the bleak truth. "Our goal is to protect you from marrying a man who has a disposition of that kind." I felt satisfied with her comment as I was confident in Henry's kind and gentle demeanor.

My face raised in elation when I caught sight of the cottage. From a stranger's viewpoint, I am sure Cliffside seems nothing more than a minute square structure with a quaint garden, but it means immeasurably more to me. The wild shrubs and vines that have meandered their way up to my bedroom window waved in the breeze, beckoning me to come and finish my slumber. This has been my cozy home, a place where my aunt's cheerful laughter emulates forth in the evening, complimenting my uncle's booming voice as we all sit in the library. The smell of countryside herbs and flowers lines the hallways constantly, and my nose recognizes Alice's warm savory recipes from the kitchen almost instantly. I could smell our breakfast right now, and it made my stomach growl in anticipation.

We returned to our warm abode and filled our aching stomachs with Alice's scrumptious sustenance. After that need was satisfied, I could barely sit upright in my chair, and both my aunt and uncle admonished me to return to bed. I breathed in the scent of cotton sheets and fresh lavender as I entered my bedroom. The drapes were still drawn with small sun beams peeking through, casting a dark shadow about the room that induced sleepiness. I crawled into bed and fell fast asleep as soon as my head hit my soft, fluffy pillow.

 C&

Adelia Ansley.   Mrs. Adelia Ansley.   Mr. and Mrs. Henry Ansley

That looks so becoming, I thought to myself as I scrawled out my potential future names. It had such a pleasant sound to it, Adelia Ansley, with my first initial matching the last initial.

"Adelia?" My aunt quipped.

I quickly scribbled over the married names that I had mindlessly written and reticently looked up from my sketchbook. My aunt was holding out the cup of tea that she had promised to retrieve for me while I had embarrassingly become distracted by my daydreaming.

"Thank you." I flashed her a quick smile and tried to pretend that I had not been doing anything awkward.

"Trying to do some sketches?" Aunt Leah looked at me intently with her intuitive gaze, and I knew that she absolutely could tell that I had not been drawing.

"Yes." I nervously tucked my hair behind my ear and took my teacup.

"Here you go, love." My aunt turned toward my uncle and offered him his cup of tea.

"Thank you." He smiled at Aunt Leah and took her hand as she sat back down in her chair alongside his.

We were sitting in our library during a blissful summer afternoon, quietly reading and enjoying each other's company. It was the beginning of July, and the months were dragging on forever. It was an unusually warm day for our coastal town, and my mind was easily growing bored. I glanced back over to my aunt and uncle and smiled at their peaceful presence. They were sitting beside each other, reading simultaneously in silent lucidity. My Aunt Leah has dark soft blonde hair, while Uncle Richard has gray flecks coursing through his once dark hair, giving him a distinguished look. Aunt Leah is the sweetest person to be in company with, but she does have a feisty spirit and a boisterous laugh. My uncle has always said that he fell in love with Aunt Leah's laugh and personality. I am fond of my relationship with my uncle as well, for he treats me sincerely and has allowed me the full use of his library which contains topics such as poetry, history, geography, and social ethics. Secretly, I have almost thought of them as my parents even though I refer to them as my aunt and uncle. Gratefulness settles in my heart when I take the time to reflect on the outstanding example they have modeled regarding how to properly show kindness and respect to others during everyday interactions.

Of course, Henry continues to pervade my thoughts constantly, and I eagerly hope he will be my future partner in life. I have encountered him several times since the ball, including town hall dances and dinner parties. Through several dances with him and typical conversations, I have surmised that nothing has changed in our status, but I earnestly believe I am a favorite for him. I was deprived of seeing him a few nights ago at the Camden's dinner party, to my dejection. I implored Edith to ask Oliver about Henry's whereabouts that night. I will see her again at Clara's garden tea party in a few days, and surely she will satisfy my curiosity then.

When my uncle heard me sigh with restlessness he proceeded to engage me. "Is this a rather boring way to spend a Saturday afternoon Adelia?"

"Oh no! I usually enjoy our quiet reading sessions, but I do not currently feel like picking up a book."

My uncle started to tease me. "Have you finally grown tired of reading countless novels filled with romantic couples and relationships?"

"Do not disrespect my passion for the works of Jane Austen and Brontë!" I rebuffed with mock hurt.

"You enjoy those stories because you hope your romantic endeavors will mirror those of the heroines." He continued much to my discomfiture. I have not openly discussed my regard for Henry in front of my uncle, but I have a sneaking suspicion that my aunt has filled him in on some of the details.

Aunt Leah elbowed him. "Richard! Do not make fun of her!"

"I grew up with two younger sisters, I believe I have some insight into the female psyche, not all, but some." He smiled at both of us while Leah and I exchanged a knowing womanly gaze.

"Well, Adelia, if you need a new novel that is similar to the genre of romance, you should try this book that I recently finished." My aunt handed me a thick, dark-covered bound novel entitled North and South. I picked it up, inhaling the essence of printery ink, glue, and fresh paper. Is there anything in the world that smells better than a brand-new book?

"The young woman, Margaret, reminds me of you, Adelia. She travels with her parents to the city, where she learns of the cruel and injustice ways of labor and social class. I think you will identify with her morals and spirit." She explained the basic summary of the book in just a way to whet my appetite for the story. "And of course, she has to contend with the difficult Mr. Thornton."

I love the excitement and pleasure of starting a new novel! "Thank you, that sounds most intriguing. I wish I could whisk away to someplace new and thrilling."

"To which faraway land?" Uncle Richard inquired, stirring up the knowledge and facts for geography that I had learned from his textbooks in Cliffside's library.

"Well in a far-reaching scope, I suppose the ideal would be a tour of Europe, I would get to see France and everything in between." I knew the likelihood of that holiday happening without marrying a wealthy upper-class gentleman was second to none, so I settled for something else. "But honestly, I do believe it would be gratifying to go to London, in the city."

"Remember, you do have your cousin Helena, who lives in London. She might be willing to host you for a holiday sometime." Aunt Leah prompted my memory. Helena is the daughter of my uncle's oldest sister, and she is several years older than me. Growing up, I used to see my cousins several times a year when my uncle's sisters would come to visit us. Helena and I always got along the best, and I attended her wedding a few years ago. She currently lives in London with her husband and two children.

I made a mental note to pen a note to Helena, as we usually fall out of communication easily. "I am sure that would be delightful, I have been feeling restless lately. I wish something invigorating would happen!" I forlornly expressed.

"Maybe something will." My aunt said while winking at me over her teacup which was delicately raised up to her smiling lips.

I ducked my uncontrollable grin behind my watercolor paper as I understood her secret message. Sometimes I wonder what the

general populous would think of me if they truly knew how many
of my waking hours, and sleeping nights, were spent contemplating
Henry Ansley.

Several days later found me sitting in the Ansley's spacious and
colorful garden. I had come alone as my aunt was occupied helping
a family with their sick children. The first thing I did was greet Clara
who was bouncing between her guests as the young socialite hostess
that she was playing that afternoon. Her mother was surveying the
interactions while talking amongst the older women in attendance.
I dashed over to Edith who was already sitting with a cup of tea and
chatting with her cousin, Eliza, who was visiting for the summer.

Edith saw me approaching and seemed to brush off her cousin
quickly. "Yes, we will talk more, but go get a cup of tea, and maybe
mingle with a few of the other ladies you have been introduced to?"
She gave Eliza a forceful tap on the shoulder and called me over.
"Adelia!"

"Hello! How are you?" I inquired and then quickly asked a
follow-up question. "What is it? You look as if you can hardly contain
something."

Edith pursed her lips while trying not to squeal. "Oh, do sit
down and then I will tell you!" I obeyed her order and leaned in close,
as I could infer it was something secretive. My mind immediately
wondered if she was going to inform me of some tidbit of news about
Henry.

"Do you remember the evening party at my family's home the
other night?"

"Of course."

"Well, the Ansley's stayed extremely late, and Oliver and I were together almost all night. Around midnight, he suggested we get a breath of fresh air, and we stepped out onto the gazebo covering. He took my hand and asked me to marry him. He asked me to marry him, Adelia!" She finished with a flourished whisper. Her story shook me to the core. Edith was engaged.

"And what did you say to him?" I said breathlessly as my throat seemed paper dry and closed.

Her eyes grew wide as she chided me. "As if you need to even ask that! I said yes Adelia, and I truly feel like the luckiest, happiest girl in the world!" She exclaimed in still a hushed whisper tone. "He has already gained my father's permission for my hand, and we shall announce it soon."

"I am immensely delighted for you, my dear friend!" I hugged her while trying to mask the anxiety that was beginning to brew in my conflicting thoughts. Thankfully, she was so focused on her own fortuitous turn of events that she did not notice or acknowledge the emotion that may have manifested on my face.

"I can barely imagine that in a few months I will be Mrs. Ansley!" She gasped.

"It is very exciting!" I grinned. "Your dreams and wishes have come true."

"We will have to discuss more in a little bit. I must go check on Eliza, as she is dreadfully shy and somewhat awkward." She stood up while looking around for her cousin. "Oh, Adelia, I really am ever so happy!"

I pressed my lips into a smile as she walked away, but I felt more nervous than ever. I was genuinely elated for Edith, but this news was a fresh reminder that my attempt at romance had thus far not been very progressive. I had also forgotten to ask her where Henry had been the past few weeks, and that question kept gnawing at my mind. I was sipping my tea while mulling over these thoughts when I was gently pulled out of my haze by Clara. She had come over to chat with me, and it was most welcome. After talking about the usual feminine topics of dresses, dances, and decorum, she spoke of something most interesting.

"Well with Henry gone away to London, I find myself growing increasingly bored throughout the day. I always forget how easy it is to miss one of my brothers." Clara spoke nonchalantly and nibbled on a pastry.

"Gone away to London?" I echoed her statement before I could stop myself.

She looked up from her food. "Yes, he has been gone for a whole fortnight now. He traveled to visit with our friends in the city. Do you know, Henry was acting so very strange before he left? He seemed distracted and evermore engrossed in his thoughts."

Could Henry have been thinking about me? I wondered at the probability of it as Clara was describing Henry exhibiting lovesick symptoms. "Could he have been anxious about his trip to the city?" I wanted additional clarification.

"No, he is never concerned about travel, and besides, he is amongst people he has known his entire life." Clara confirmed what I was hoping his city social circles would be. Most likely he was enjoying company with other young men who were his close friends, and with fate on my side, he would not be introduced to too many new young women.

I wished I could squeeze more information out of Clara about Henry, but I did not want her to detect any attachment on my part. I turned our discussion back to small talk. "Have you enjoyed your summer in Hastings?"

"Yes, I have! I was expecting it to be dull here, but I have been pleasantly surprised at the social events and interesting people that Hastings has had to offer." She lifted her cup of tea and then her words registered. "Oh, but I hope I have not offended you by admitting my false assumption of deciding your town would be a bore!"

"No, you are fine." I reassured her. "Honestly, I myself have moments when I wish my town had more adventure, but I am glad you have found it pleasant." She agreed and we continued to talk until we parted ways as she had to continue mingling with her other guests. I determined I was ready for a light refreshment along with my fresh cup of tea, so I stood up as well and walked over to a table filled with food. I felt deflated as I saw Agnes and Emma Langston once again huddled up by the table, whispering in low tones. I was beginning to wonder if they ever talked to anyone else at gatherings since they always seem more occupied with scheming together. Deciding that they would be the ones to move along, I continued my path. Shockingly, they chose to acknowledge me.

"Adelia!" Emma started. "How are you doing?"

"I am quite well." I barely addressed her greeting and continued to ignore.

"Was that Clara talking to you a few minutes ago? What did she have to say?" Agnes prodded.

So, this was their game. Pretending to be interested, in order to gain tantalizing details about the Ansley's. "The two of us discussed so many things, it is hard to pinpoint exactly what you are asking about." I answered generically.

"Did she mention anything about her siblings? Particularly where one of her older brothers has been recently?" Agnes tried to clarify while smiling and acting coy.

"Oh, you are asking after Mr. Henry?" They nervously giggled as I continued. "Why do you assume that I would have any knowledge of his whereabouts? I am actually surprised that you came to speak with me at all. You are usually more than happy to insult me behind my back, and you have made it most clear that you have no interest in being genuine friends."

What I said must have been so out of character for myself, that they both stood there in a shocked state, unsure of how to respond. They knew I was right though, and I was not willing to tolerate their rude antics.

"Have a good rest of the afternoon." I smiled sweetly and turned to go back to my spot, where Edith had rejoined my group. Settling in under the cool shade of the hedge along with the other young women, I felt content and savored the remainder of my stay in the company of my true friends as well as the delicious food with tea. Of course, it was equally satisfying to secretly relish the stunned faces of Agnes and Emma Langston at the rebuff I had dealt them earlier. I could not help but imagine a similar expression developing across their pallid features when in the future they heard of my engagement to Henry Ansley. One can only hope.

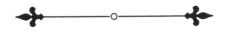

Chapter 6

Naturally, the next event I was looking forward to would have been Edith's engagement party. I reasoned that Henry would not miss his own brother's gathering, so it would be the first I would have seen of him in about a month. I was anticipating the thrill of his presence, and Edith's wedding would also be coming soon, by the autumn no doubt.

I was experiencing the same emotions I felt when preparing for the ball back in May, but somehow, I was more anxious, because I was eager to be near Henry again. I fussed over my outfit for the evening, wanting to look as beautiful as possible, imagining our conversation after a period of separation. After all, absence makes the heart grow fonder!

And here I was in that familiar state of mind, arriving at the Ansley's, great expectations for the evening, hopes and dreams still abounding. He was there, standing with his family, looking handsome as ever, while the guests came into the room. Our names were announced, and I was awaiting a glance towards my direction, a smile, anything.

Imagine my unease rising when Henry did not even look up at me when I entered, or as I walked by him. This was not typical behavior, he used to always glance after me when we passed by each other or acknowledge me with a greeting. I was unsure of how to act, for not knowing why he was ignoring me was torture. It got worse as the evening progressed because as each hour passed, my interaction with Henry had still been about naught. No conversation, no eye contact, no smiles, absolutely nothing.

This issue did not improve at all, as there were several situations at the gathering that would have warranted an easy opening for conversation together. For instance, when I went up to talk to Edith and Oliver, Henry and Clara were already engaged in conversation with them, but just as I approached the group, Henry turned and left. Later, when card game groups were being set up, there was an obvious open spot for partnering next to me, but Henry deliberately chose to sit at a different table on the other side of the room, where his mother and sister were stationed.

My overactive mind instantly started to make up reasons to account for his behavior that evening. Maybe he was tired from his trip to London. Perhaps he was feeling anxiety since his younger brother will be getting married before him. Could he be facing the impending impact of his brother's nuptials, wondering if the pressure will now be on him as the oldest son to choose a marriage partner? My time during the meal was spent pondering this predicament, and I did not know exactly what to believe. Edith could not be a source of help or confidence, as I was at an event in honor of her and Oliver, and I should have been focused on the happy couple. All I could do was smile through my angst and attempt to show attention to my sparkling friend Edith during one of her happiest moments, but inside I was absolutely miserable.

When I went home that night, I was still unsettled, and I had a strange dream as I was trying to sleep. In this dream, I saw Henry holding hands with a faceless girl, but I could not determine if I was an onlooker, or the girl, because she had the same long and dark curly hair as mine. A pregnant Edith and her husband Oliver passed by Henry and the girl, commenting on their upcoming marriage union.

I woke up confused, trying to decipher my dream in the still, dark night. I rested my head on my knees as I was beginning to feel the long-term effects that the stress and frustration of wishing for Henry had on my well-being. Every move he made, each facial expression, I was always analyzing him to try to comprehend his body language and mood. He had an unspoken power over me, and I was starting to fully understand the hold it had on me daily. If only he would end my agony by revealing his true feelings!

I concluded that the dream was nothing more than my inner self trying to sort out my problems during my sleeping hours. The girl with Henry in my dream must have been me as I was not left with an eerie or despairing feeling when I awoke, and if anything, it seemed that other people were commenting on our match as a couple. I only wish I had recognized that my dream proved to be more foreboding than I had initially thought.

The rest of the summer went by quickly, filled with the excitement of helping plan Edith's wedding. I saw little of Henry, and I again heard that he had traveled to London during August. It was early into September, a few weeks away from the wedding, when Clara and I were talking, that she accidentally slipped by sharing a major detail about Henry's future plans. We were sitting with Edith in my garden, helping her discuss the details for the gathering after her ceremony.

"It will be thrilling to attend a wedding again!" Clara had exclaimed. "I believe I was young at the last wedding I went to, and

I do not remember much. It should be exciting to see some of our extended family there, including Henry and his new lady friend."

The blood in my veins turned icy cold.

"Henry is courting someone?" Edith asked while looking over at me with concerned eyes.

"Oh no!" Clara covered her mouth with her hands. "That is not common knowledge. I was not supposed to say anything!"

"But is he seeing someone?" I needed an answer, and I was praying that I had misheard her words.

"Well, I can only assume she will be coming to the wedding, so I guess it does not matter if you ladies know." She started to explain. "Henry started courting Monique Alarie earlier this summer. The Alarie's are a wealthy family in London that we have known for years." Her tone was so nonchalant, she had no idea that she was speaking words that were breaking my heart.

"I think he wanted to keep it discreet for now, as not to intrude or draw attention away from you and Oliver, Edith." Clara was still giving us details of Henry's relationship, and it was making my stomach queasy. "But they have known each other for so long, and our parents greatly approve. Adelia, are you well? You look quite pale." Clara had noticed my shocked demeanor. Edith also looked distressed as she knew how my secret admiration for Henry might be affected by this news.

"I am fine." I managed to stammer.

Thankfully, Clara stopped rambling on about her eldest brother and moved onto a new subject. However, I retained absolutely no information from the rest of the conversation between my two friends. I sat in a daze, nodding every so often to appear present, and trying to smile as part of my cheerful facade. It was later when the girls were getting ready to leave and Clara had walked over to admire some of my planted flowers, that Edith spoke up.

"Adelia, are you despaired over this information about Henry? We do not even truly know if it is true!" She exclaimed.

"Why would Clara embellish what is going on with her brother?" I asked simply.

"It is most likely a rumor! She said that Monique is supposedly the daughter of a family they have all known for many years. It is the parents; the parents are hoping Henry and Monique will make a match!" Edith had already concocted this conclusion in her mind. "I have seen the way he looks at you, do not be concerned. It is simply a case of a forward flirting woman, but your Henry is not interested."

"Maybe you are right. I probably should not overreact straight away. I have always been aware of the connection Henry and I share."

"Exactly! Besides, I will ask Oliver for further details and then inform you. Surely he will clarify exactly what Clara meant." She bid me goodbye with a promise to update me soon, and the two girls walked out together.

All I could do was hold my breath and hope that Clara was sincerely mistaken. I soothed myself by replaying Edith's words in my mind. She was going to confer with Oliver and would update me soon. Everything would be joyous at the wedding, and with Oliver and Edith married, Henry would feel comfortable beginning a relationship with me. I smiled and my head nodded in agreement with my own silent thoughts.

ॐ

To my dismay, Edith did not explain any details she gained from Oliver nor update me about Henry. In fact, I barely saw or spoke to her until the wedding day. I had a sneaking suspicion she was avoiding me on purpose. It did not help that I was busy teaching at Ms. Lynn's, and she was preparing for last-minute wedding details along with packing for her honeymoon trip.

I peered into the mirror after I had dressed for Edith's wedding. My new lilac-colored bridesmaid dress was beautiful and soft, and I had enjoyed sewing it with my aunt. Out of habit, I bit my lip and spun a strand of hair through my fingers as I pondered what I might see at the gathering. My courage rose when the morning sun peeked out from behind a typical coastal cloud and shone through to beam upon my face. It left me feeling rosy and I stubbornly decided that I was going to have a conversation with Henry at the party, even if I had to force him to engage with me. It was time to see Edith off into her new life and push my future forward.

We arrived with a good amount of time before the ceremony, and I was eager to check in with Edith. A few minutes before the allotted time of the marriage ceremony, I stationed myself a few paces behind where I was going to enter, and I started scanning the rows of people, searching for Monique, the lady whom Edith and I had talked about. The Ansley's had a considerable number of guests on their side of the two families, and Henry was going to be with his brother as the marriage took place, so it was hard to determine if there was an unrelated girl to the Ansley family in attendance.

I forced myself to focus on the happy couple, and the wedding proceedings went smoothly. I genuinely believed Edith and Oliver were filled with fondness for each other, and it made my heart swell to see my friend jubilant and triumphant over her romance. The ceremony led into an afternoon gathering in celebration. My purpose shifted to myself now that Edith was married. I was going to use the afternoon to assess what was going on with Henry and make sure a future with him was still attainable.

My stomach rolled uneasily as if it would flip entirely when I finally did locate him, for I saw he was standing next to an unknown yet beautiful young woman. She had an aristocratic nature as she was talking to an older woman, along with an open, fluttering fan and sepia curls that floated down the back of her elaborate pastel rose dress. What was more alarming was her left hand that rested on Henry's forearm, dangerously close to his wrist and hand. Taking a breath to encourage valiance, I walked over to approach him while the young woman was still focused on the other guest. He saw me approach, and in that moment, I observed him gently, but briskly, pull away from the young woman's hand. She looked up at him with a flash of confusion but continued laughing and talking to the older woman.

"Henry." I began quietly so that only he would hear. "I must talk to you."

He barely looked at me and responded with a frosty tone. "In a moment Miss Hadlee."

My lungs deflated when he called me Miss Hadlee. Henry had insisted we address each other by our first names at the ball. What had changed so that he was uncomfortable calling me Adelia? Half a minute later, the young woman having finished her conversation, turned back to Henry and now me as well since I was still standing there, completely stupefied.

"Henry, who is this?" She asked looking at me directly, her fan now slowly waving in front of her face.

Henry avoided acknowledging me and answered her in a dismissive tone. "Oh, this is one of my sister's friends, Miss Hadlee." Just his sister's friend? This was going horribly wrong.

She smiled and introduced herself. "Hello. I am Lady Monique Alarie." She spoke clearly, with a distinct French accent, an element adding to her sophisticated persona. "It is nice to meet you, Miss Hadlee." She said, obviously waiting for me to respond. Instead, I continued to stare at the two of them, particularly Henry who was trying to do anything but look at us two women. The next moment another guest walked by and addressed both Henry and Monique clearly.

My ears picked up the words of the excited woman. "What a wonderful wedding, wouldn't you agree? It is encouraging to see one of my nephews married, but I hear that we might have another Ansley wedding soon!" The chattering woman smiled at Monique who laughed and used her smooth conversation skills to charm Henry's relative. Henry gave me an almost penitent glance, but I felt utterly humiliated.

"I was looking for Clara." I lied with downcast eyes, and turned from him, blinking back tears. I hurriedly tried to walk away with trembling knees, leading myself to where my aunt was sitting independently in a quiet corner.

"Adelia, whatever is the matter?" My aunt exclaimed as soon as she saw my face. There was never any fooling her.

"I was just speaking to Henry's Lady Monique who he is courting." I sighed in defeat and bit my lip to suppress the sinking sorrow that was threatening to upset my moderately calm demeanor.

"Oh, Adelia!" My aunt rushed to console me. "I am so sorry. Is it certain that he is clearly involved with her?"

I nodded in agreement. "An aunt of his came up while I was in their presence and made a comment about their impending engagement. They could already be engaged for all I know."

My aunt was quiet, but also looked upset, and I knew she was trying to assess my pain. "Are you going to be alright?"

I did not even realize how much it hurt at that moment, because I felt strangely numb and in disbelief regarding what had just transpired. "I do not know. I cannot discuss it right now."

She nodded but continued to observe me and I could feel empathy exuding out of her silence. People around me were lighthearted and cheery over the wedding and I was pretending to be one of them, smiling to keep myself from crying.

I was outside, taking in the warm evening air as I contemplated the events from the afternoon. I slowly sat back down after walking the length of our garden. I was dreading going inside for supper, as I felt quiet and calm for the moment. Sorrow weighed heavy on my chest, and I knew what would happen if I was forced to express my emotion.

My mind was trying to play tricks on me, and in denial, I wanted to believe that somehow what I had seen earlier in the day was false and Henry was not truly in a relationship with Monique. I replayed him bristling away from her grasp over and over, and in my mind,

I deemed it as purposeful. He never introduced her to me properly, she had to announce herself. It was almost as if he felt awkward in her presence.

"Adelia."

I looked up quickly at my aunt walking towards me. "Hello." I greeted.

"There you are. I came to find you." She explained softly. "How are you doing?"

I was going to attempt to control myself, but her simple question broke open the flood of tears. "Not good." I sobbed while wet drops slipped down both of my cheeks. I continued to cry silently while my aunt sat with me for comfort. I finally breathed out an honest question. "Was it ever real? At any time did I have a true chance with him?"

She reached for my hand and then gave me her opinion on Henry. "It is disappointing because he did not understand the value of what your companionship would have been to him. That is his loss Adelia, and you need to remember that."

Aunt Leah had not acknowledged if it was a real relationship though. I knew the answer deep down. "I am such a fool!" I exclaimed in despair. "I envisioned it in my mind. That was all it was. He never took me seriously as a romantic partner." This revelation sent me into another string of sobs and sniffles.

"But you are not completely to blame!" Aunt Leah tried to reason me out of my self-deprecation. "What is a young woman to think if a single man is flirting with her and stands up to dance first dances with her? Please, Adelia, give yourself a measure of grace, you are young and inexperienced. You felt strongly for him and stayed true to your heart. I am deeply sorry this was the result."

I tried to steady my breathing as she continued speaking. "Besides, there are plenty of other young men that you will cross paths with during your adult life. They cannot all be as inconsiderate as the eldest Ansley son." She chuckled satirically to amuse me, but I was perturbed at her remark. I did not want another young man's affection, I wanted Henry and I had yearned for his affections for a long period of time.

"Is this conversation helping at all?" My aunt was timidly smiling, but the sadness and pain from my sorrow reflected in her usual merry eyes. I perceived that she was hoping that I was feeling better. I did not know what I felt anymore. Crying always leaves me feeling weak and exhausted. I could not remember the last time that I had cried like this and released all my emotions. My aunt and uncle have always said that I was such an easy child, and an overall uplifting person to be around. I had to be fine, I have always been fine in the past.

"I suppose so." I finally answered her. She sighed and sat back, still watching me carefully. I furiously started to wipe away my moist cheeks when I saw my uncle walking out to where my aunt and I were situated. "Do I appear as if I have been bawling over a boy?" I ruefully asked Aunt Leah.

"No, you are fine. We can tell him you are tired." My aunt reassured me and smiled one last time.

"Are my two ladies getting ready for supper?" My uncle asked with his contented smile and reached for Aunt Leah's hand. Regular life was going to continue around me.

I turned the stuck knob on my bedroom door and listening as the frame uttered its familiar squeak, pressing the wood closed. I was finally alone, by myself. I had retreated from my family after the meal, explaining my fatigue required an immediate removal to bed. I glanced into my room that had been so inviting before, a place where I could dream and wish and have peace. My room appeared dark and gloomy, seemingly transposing my current disposition into my living space.

I sunk down onto my bed and winced as the pressure sent a dull ache through my temples. I had developed a tension pain in my head from my episode of crying. I dropped onto my pillow, lost in my mind and feelings of emptiness. In a strange way, I wanted to cry over him more, but I felt as if my tears were dissolved. I knew I was going to have to give all of it up, everything about him that lived in me, but I wanted to use my breath and voice to scream the intensity of it out into the world. However, at the same time, I was a mute, these thoughts confined to the cage that was my active mind.

There was nothing for me to do other than go to sleep and hope for more coherence in the morning. Numbly, I took off my day dress and slipped into my soft worn nightgown. I had my fingers engaged in sweeping through my curls when my eyes caught sight of the seashells that Henry had given to me that one day down at the beach. That day seemed like it had been several years ago instead of a few months earlier. I had removed the seashells from my bookshelf and strategically laid them on my bedside table in order to see them when I was falling asleep. My fingers shook as I slowly reached out to grab them. I wanted those perfect, beautiful little reminders to disappear. Anger welled up in my chest and I deftly stomped over to my window. I opened it, letting the night air travel in, and raised my clenched fist. I pitched them out and heard a series of satisfying thumps as they scattered onto the stones and grass outside.

I was going to have to cut away anything that reminded me of him, but I could not do it all immediately. In that instant, I had a flash of a memory from my dance with him, the touch of his hand, the warmth in his eyes, his shy smile. It caused a piercing, hollow ache to roll through my chest like a wave and then crash into my head. The tide came in, and tears were stinging at my eyes again. I swiftly moved back to my bed to smother myself under the blankets and pillows to silence my echoing sobs and sharp breaths.

My final thought as I drifted off to sleep that night was that I was never going to allow another man to make me feel the emotions that Henry Ansley had caused me to experience. I was sealing off my heart, rolling a huge stone across the entrance to guard my feelings and lock away my regard for romantic love.

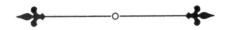

Chapter 7

My misery materialized itself in the fog that rolled in on the cold autumn mornings at Cliffside and lingered throughout the daylight hours. Henry had been a part of me for so long that I could barely remember how to function without thinking of him or the hope of our budding romance. The aching emptiness would not depart from me, resulting in days that blurred by as I fragilely tried to pick up the broken pieces of my heart. It did not help for the people in my social groups to be completely absorbed by any and every interesting tidbit about couples or matchmaking and spread them amongst their various audiences for everyone to hear. The constant chattering made me exasperated and greatly affected my mood and behavior for the worse. I realized how contemptuous I was being when I was interacting with one of my pupils on a particularly droll afternoon in the beginning of October.

"But why does the letter C sometimes sound like the letter S?" Sarah, my student of six asked.

"You pronounce C as the S sound if the C follows a vowel, usually E, I, or Y." I explained.

She looked at me as if I were speaking a foreign language. "What does that mean? What are the vowels again?"

"Must I explain everything twice Sarah?" I sighed with a tone of annoyance. "I need you to listen when I am teaching you."

She looked up at me in shock at my reprimand and I instantly felt remorse for my lapse in patience. "I am trying Miss Adelia." Sarah sulked and looked down at the floor.

"I know, I am sorry." I kneeled to face her at eye level. "I did not sleep well last night, and I fear I am ill-tempered this morning. Would you like me to explain it once more?" She nodded with a hesitant smile, and we continued the lesson without any other mishaps.

After my teaching session, I went for a walk towards town for something unusual to do out of my typical weekday routine. My favorite place to go was the small book shop in the middle of the main street. I entered through the threshold and a tiny bell sounded off above me to alert the shopkeeper of customers.

"Hello, Adelia! What can I help you with today?" Mrs. Bradley was working the counter for her husband when I entered.

"I thought I would browse for a few minutes, Mrs. Bradley." I answered with a smile. She nodded silently and went back to the register. She understood my love for books and the peacefulness of the store. I moved to the shelves filled with new publications and started looking through the titles. Reading the spines on the books and seeing the varying hues of the book bindings grounded me as I thumbed through a few of the books. The bell sounded off again and I heard the obnoxious voice of Agnes Langston. I quickly flattened myself into a blind spot between two bookshelves, hoping that she would not walk past me. Her mother, Mariah, was with her instead of her sister.

"Which author did he mention he enjoys reading?" Mariah asked a few bookshelves over, already seeming overwhelmed at the never-ending aisles of books there were available to look through.

"They are all the same!" Agnes rolled her eyes. "Why couldn't Tom be more interested in the usual manly things such as hunting? I think it may have been Charles Dickens."

Her flippant attitude made me chuckle to myself. Agnes has been trying to get close to Tom Dawson recently, and I guess her mother's latest scheme was for her insipid daughter to feign interest in anything that the young man is engrossed by.

"Here are a few. Which title was his favorite, Agnes?" Mariah impatiently addressed her obviously bored daughter.

"I do not remember. I became distracted and stopped listening after a while." She exclaimed in dismay. "It is exhausting to try to keep an eligible suitor interested."

"You must remain at it a little longer; I believe you have a good chance with this young man." Mariah spoke.

"Yes, well it is not my fault that every young man I have tried to pursue ends up already having a romantic connection!" I secretly disagreed with that statement. Agnes continued. "It was ever so infuriating that handsome Henry had a fancy city girl waiting for him. He would have been such an agreeable suitor." She sighed.

A familiar dull, aching pain stabbed at my heart at the mere mention of Henry's name.

"It is vexing because I have it on good authority that they are announcing their engagement and then will be staying in Hastings after they get married. What could be the reason for that if they have connections to London? If you are not single, then move along, we have no use for you." Mariah spoke whilst balancing several books in her stout arms. "We will buy a couple of Dickens novels and then you will have several things to discuss with Tom."

"Mother, will I have to read all of those books? It will take me forever." Agnes was appalled at what her mother was suggesting.

"Would it really cause your death to read at least one book, child?" Mariah was becoming ever more exasperated.

"It might." Agnes moped. They moved forward to the register and left within a matter of minutes. I slowly slipped out of my hiding spot and decided to make my way home.

"Did you find anything of interest, Adelia?" Mrs. Bradley asked as I passed by.

"I most certainly did, just nothing of the book variety. See you next time." I forced out and left the shop.

I trudged home, taking no delight in the trees that had shifted from brushy green to crisp colors of yellow, orange, and red. The angst was welling up in my chest again as I thought over what Mrs. Mariah Langston had said. I do not try to believe the idle gossip of anyone, but I knew of the impending engagement of Henry and Monique. I dreaded the idea of having the whole town whispering about it, congratulations floating on the wind, and seeing the two of them after they were married with any regularity. I stomped into the entry of our home to take off my shoes and hang up my coat. I entered the study looking for my sketching supplies for a much-needed distraction. My aunt was reading on the chaise while a fire warmed up the room.

"Hello. How are you?" She asked cheerfully.

"Fine." I responded with an edge of bitterness. I sat down with my pencils and started to harshly scribble on the paper to appear occupied.

She closed her book and regarded me skeptically. "That is not the truth. Do you want to talk about it?"

"No. Yes. I do not know." I answered, my emotions warring inside me. I focused on a small skylark perched on a branch by the window. Was it possible to feel envy over a little bird's freedom? It gets to fly wherever it wants, see whatever it wants without being beholden to anyone.

"Are you having a difficult time?" My aunt continued to probe me.

"I cannot tolerate the obsession that everyone has over a certain couple." I forbade myself to speak his name.

"Have you overheard anything in particular that caused an irritation?" My aunt asked.

"The rumor is that they will be staying here after their wedding, for whatever reason." I sighed. "I do not wish to be here; it would be tortuous for me to have to see them together for any length of time."

"She must like it in Hastings then, to want to live here." Aunt Leah concluded.

"I suppose." I replied. "I wish I could run away from this tempestuous storm that I call life."

"I am sorry. I would help shield you from this storm if I could." My aunt smiled tenderly and came over to hug me. "Remember, after a storm, usually the sky opens, and radiant sunlight breaks forth. You just need to wait for the sunlight, Adelia. The storm clouds will soon pass."

"How long will this last? Why does it have to sting so much?" I needed answers.

"I do not know. You felt intensely, so of course, it will not go away quickly. Adelia, I know it hurts, but I need you to look at this as a character-building moment in your life. Learning from sorrow and hard times will help you gain resilience."

I nodded and turned back to my sketchbook to try and draw the small skylark from the window. Cook Alice poked her head in at that exact moment bringing in a small stack of letters.

"The mail was delivered." She said and left the various sized envelopes on the side table by the door.

My aunt walked over and started sorting through the trove of letters. "This one is for you Adelia. From Helena." She handed me a white envelope written with a cursive script. I had forgotten I had written my cousin a few weeks back and was awaiting a reply. I ripped it open and started reading.

October 1st, 1857

Dear Adelia,

I must apologize for this late reply, I have been so busy! We are well, but my recently hired governess quit, which has caused an amount of strife in my life! Alfred, who you remember is six years old, drove the governess to her wit's end with his mischievous antics, and I am afraid he received no education the one month that she was employed. His younger sister Eleanor made little to no improvement with her reading skills whatsoever, and I am not good at helping her. This leads me to a genius idea I had when I remembered your letter. I know that you teach and tutor girls with literacy and I am sure you are exceptionally good at working with children. Would you consider traveling to London to be my children's informal governess? Alfred will be going to school in the next year or so, but I need to get him used to the idea of sitting still and listening, and I am sure Eleanor would do well under your tutelage. And when you are not teaching the children, I can show you London on the evenings and weekends. We can offer you more than what your earned wage is now, plus a bonus if you can arrive within the next few weeks... Please say yes! Write me back soon with a reply. Sending my love to Uncle Richard and Aunt Leah.

Sincerely,

Helena Braxton.

"What does she write? How is she doing?" My aunt asked.

"I think it may be the beginning of the sun breaking through the storm clouds." I handed her the letter to read. I started to gleefully smile for the first time in weeks. I finally had an opportunity to go somewhere interesting!

I breathed a sigh of relief as I sat down on the train and looked out the window. My aunt and uncle waved to me from the platform, and I smiled, waving goodbye one last time. Fittingly, I was setting off for my journey the day that I turned twenty-one, which was a gloriously free October morning. It seemed to encourage me to look at this life change as the start of a fresh year. A new year of my life, free from heartbreak and depressing thoughts.

I recalled my aunt's words as she saw me off at the train station. After hugging me and telling me how much she was going to miss me she gave me a piece of advice.

"Adelia, I am glad that this invitation coincidentally arrived during you grieving the loss of that potential relationship, but I do want to admonish you to not completely push this experience out of your mind. It happened for a reason, this is how we learn, and you should continue to reflect and glean any insight that it has had on you."

I nodded, more soberly, and agreed. "I understand what you are saying Aunt Leah, and I will keep that in mind. Thank you for being my advisor, amongst many other roles." I told her.

"Of course! Please, write to me whenever you feel up to it, or need my advice on anything that happens while you are away."

"I will."

She handed me another small bag. "Here are a few remedies and oils for you if you feel unwell while you are away." Aunt Leah embraced me. "I am going to miss you, Adelia."

"Thank you. I will miss you too." I smiled bravely as she cast one last loving and motherly gaze upon me. With that, I turned around and boarded the train.

Reflecting on that conversation, I realized how in the last few years of my young adult life I had sometimes taken for granted my aunt's wise advice and gentle counsel. The last month or so had been spent chiding myself for not listening to her meek warnings about pining away for someone who I barely knew or letting my heart fall so far, so easily. But I did fall, and now I had to pay the price for my borrowed heart.

Musings such as these grew deeper in my thoughts as the train departed and set off for my grand destination. A small fire started burning in my chest as I truly realized that I was not completely at fault for my ridiculous infatuation with Henry Ansley. A lightening of memories flashed in my mind causing the insidious ache to attempt to settle on me, but I chose to ignore it this time. His flirting, complementing my eyes, talking openly to me, smiles and lingering stares from across the room, giving me seashells to remember him by. He had encouraged me to a certain degree, and I fell all over him like a small pup trailing after its master. Never again, would that situation repeat itself in my life story. I was going to take control over my own feelings and do my best to ignore the young male population entirely for now.

Satisfied with this epiphanic conclusion and the heartfelt promise made to myself, I wondered if I could finally start moving on. This was a new chapter, a fresh start, and I was going to take full advantage of that. Feeling resolved, I settled down into my seat and made myself comfortable for the several hour-long journey that lay ahead.

The train jolted and screeched as it pulled into the London station. Passengers started to move about in a flurry, checking to see if they had their possessions in order to disembark from the coach. I waited patiently for my turn and filed through the hallway to the exit. I reached the doorway and looked down at the steep gap between the bottom step and the train platform. The staff was unavailable to assist, busy with barking out orders and arranging luggage for unloading.

Anxiety loomed over me as people started pushing up and around the door waiting for me to step down. I clumsily tripped as the length of my legs proved inadequate to meet the gap below the step and struggled to regain my balance, to no avail. Unfortunately, in this moment, I collided with a tall person of the male persuasion, thus breaking my fall. I haphazardly landed on the platform, somehow losing hold of my suitcase as well. A pair of strong arms and hands were now wrapped firmly around my waist, helping me regain equilibrium.

"Are you alright Miss?" The hands connected to the arms gently spun me around, so I was now facing the man who had caught me. I looked up, for this person was at least another head taller than me, and I found myself gazing into a pair of sparkling sapphire eyes. "Just another day at the train station, catching a damsel in distress." The stranger exclaimed, grinning from ear to ear, flashing perfectly white teeth against the tan skin of his face, obviously thinking he was amusing.

"I am not in distress!" I scoffed and instantly felt his hands that were still resting firmly on my waist. I hurriedly pushed them off, aware of the small crowd of people that were now watching us. I felt completely embarrassed and compromised at the spectacle that I had made of myself.

"Miss, I was only trying to help. There is no need to be uncivil." His teasing tone turned more defensive.

I ignored him and turned to get my suitcase. I saw that it was missing from the spot where it had landed after my fall and whirled back around to see that the tall stranger had picked it up and was watching me intently. This man was young, at most five-and-twenty years of age with a determined look in his eyes.

"Is this yours?" He asked teasingly.

"Yes." I said curtly while reaching for my bag as he released it from his hands. "Thank you." I hurriedly curtsied and started to walk in the opposite direction of him.

"Miss! Do you not wish to know the name of your rescuer?" He was now right behind me, still intent on trying to address me.

"No, I do not actually." I heard his footsteps continuing to follow me.

"Well then, may I have your name?"

"If I did not wish to know your name, why would I want you to know mine?" I continued at a steady pace, hoping he would take a hint.

"Acting mysterious could be your ploy."

"I can assure you it is not." I kept walking.

"I do believe you owe it to me since I did save you from falling to your death." He seemed to be growing irritated at my defiance, and I did not care for his tone.

"I owe you nothing." I spun around to face him. "And besides, you exaggerate. I would not have sustained any permanent damage to my person from a small stumble off a step."

"Well, I could not have you arriving at your destination all scraped up now could I? I stepped up as a gentleman and assisted you." We were at a stand-still, staring directly into each other's eyes, neither one of us wanting to relent on our view. I purposely broke the connection and looked around the station hoping to see Helena.

"Are you looking for someone?" He asked.

"Do you always take such an eager interest in complete strangers that you may encounter at the train station?" I retorted.

"Not typically, I made the exception for you this day, so I would appreciate a name, Miss."

Why was he so determined to learn my name? It was positively infuriating. Before I could reply, another young man came up and addressed the tall stranger. "There you are, Edwin! Our train is departing, come along." The man acknowledged me with a tip of his hat and walked away, expecting Edwin to follow him. I glanced over at this Edwin fellow with a triumphant arched brow and slight smirk, for I had unintentionally learned his name without having to admit to mine.

He knew he had lost, for he looked after his friend with a glance of annoyance and defeat. He then shook his head as he took note of my triumphant expression.

"I have never been in the habit of releasing personal details to complete and total strangers Edwin. I do thank you for your assistance earlier and I now will bid you a good day." I swiftly turned on my heels and continued walking, relieved to not hear anyone following me. I thought it unlikely that I would ever see this Edwin again, and I felt very satisfied knowing that I had the upper hand in this particularly embarrassing situation.

"Adelia!"

I finally caught sight of my cousin Helena and she waved me over smiling. I rushed to embrace her.

"Hello, Helena!" I greeted, so happy to see a familiar face.

"I apologize that I am late; I had a problem with my carriage which kept me from arriving in a timely fashion." She explained and took a good look at me. "You are always so elegant and mature whenever I see you! This is going to be much fun!" I nodded and grinned, her enthusiasm energizing me. We left the station and walked to the carriage still talking and catching up.

"Who did I see talking to you a few moments ago at the station?" Helena suddenly asked. "I did not get a good look at him, but he was very tall."

"I do not really know, I mean, sort of. It was rather an uneventful side mishap that I was not expecting to encounter." I answered with bewilderment.

"Really? You must tell me all about it on our way home." She demanded. We stepped into the coach and began driving to her residence.

"How peculiar and exciting!" She exclaimed after I had finished telling her about my experience. "Being saved by an intriguing young man at the train station."

"I did not ask to be saved mind you!" I exclaimed with a laugh. "Besides, he turned somewhat brusque when I refused to continue on in conversation with him. A true gentleman would not insist on delaying a lady so they can speak with them." I said. "All right, no more of that. Tell me about the children. How are Alfred and Eleanor?"

After hearing a full report on her young son's antics, I felt somewhat intimidated, but I knew I had to be careful not to let that show when working with him. Helena was hopeful that my being an extended family member and younger in age than his previous governess might improve how he responds to learning new subjects, but I was going to remain skeptical for the time being. I already knew Eleanor was a lovely little girl with a quiet temperament and I was looking forward to what would become my new routine. Helena continued chatting as we drove through the streets of London. Looking out a small side window, my eyes drank in each passing scene from the comfort afforded inside the carriage. Crowded streets, rows of shops, and magnificent buildings. It was all new and exciting to me. We pulled up in front of an elaborate townhouse and stepped down from the coach. Helena's house servant retrieved my luggage as we walked up the front steps together and in through the front door.

"Theodore! Are you home? Alfred? Eleanor?" Helena called for her family members as we took off our coats. I heard children's feet run upstairs and descend the staircase.

"Mommy!" Eleanor called while Alfred hesitantly slinked down the stairs, aware that someone unfamiliar was in the room.

"Hello! Where is Daddy?" Helena said while picking up Eleanor and smothering her little girl with kisses.

"He is in the office." Eleanor proclaimed proudly.

"Let us go get him!" Helena said excitedly and turned back to me. "Alfred, Eleanor, this is Adelia Hadlee. She is my cousin, and she will be your new governess for now. Say hello."

"Hi." Eleanor and Alfred answered in unison, both acting shyly.

"It is nice to meet you both. I am looking forward to spending time with you." I smiled.

"You mean spending time teaching us." Alfred corrected.

"Alfred, mind your manners." His mother warned and he kept quiet.

Helena's husband came around the corner just then and the children pounced on him.

"There you are!" Helena greeted him.

"Hello love." He kissed her on the cheek and stood beside her. "Hello, Adelia. How was your journey?"

"It was interesting." I said exchanging a secret glance with Helena. "How are you?"

"I am well, just confined to working on a civil case where I am representing. It can be a bore." Theodore works as a lawyer and comes from a well-off family which explains how my cousins have come to reside in a lavishly furnished London townhouse. "So, you have come to teach our little ragamuffins? Good luck with that!" He teased while ruffling his daughter's hair.

"Theodore, do not scare her away completely before she has time to settle in!" Helena laughed. "Come along Adelia, let me give you a tour of the house and show you to your room where you can freshen up before supper."

Once I had viewed numerous rooms, along with an impressive dining space, she brought me to the guest bedroom on the second floor.

"And this is your room!" Helena announced.

I stood in the spacious room looking around in awe. The four-poster bed was decorated with an elegant duvet and a beautifully arranged cascade of pillows in various shapes and sizes. A dressing table with a long mirror hung parallel to the bed, and a petite writing desk had been neatly tucked into the corner next to the largest window so one could easily write by the natural light flooding into the inviting room. A small fireplace stood in the middle of the center wall to provide warmth on winter nights.

"It is perfect. Thank you so much." I let out a contented sigh while peering out the wide brocade paneled windows overlooking the greenspace at the back of the property.

"Hopefully, you will adjust to your new routine and enjoy your time here. The occupants of Hastings were not too disappointed to lose you were they?" Helena asked.

I knew my aunt and uncle were naturally going to miss me, but I would see them occasionally when they came to visit. Ms. Lynn had been devasted when she learned of my plans, and she vowed she would never appreciate another teacher more than me. A few of my pupils shed tears on my shoulder as I embraced them on my last day, but I tried to reassure them that whomever Ms. Lynn hired next was worthy of their respect and full cooperation. Edith was very consumed with her new married life, but she offered that we could write to each other, and Clara's friendship was promised the same fate. Other than those few people, I was definitely not going to miss the endless memories that haunted Hastings at present.

I summed my feelings up into a short reply. "I am sure they will manage the loss. I am certainly going to enjoy a welcoming break from the comings and goings of small-town life for now."

Helena's eyebrows upturned. "It sounds like there could be a story hidden somewhere in that reply."

I shrugged dismissively and reached for my luggage to start unpacking.

"Well, supper is at half-past seven, and we agreed you will start teaching the children on Monday. That gives you a little time to get settled." Helena started for the door. "Oh, and Adelia, we are invited to an informal evening dinner party the week after next. I told the host I have a relation staying with us at present and she said you are welcome to come!"

"I do not know if I will be ready for social events quite yet." I answered while hanging up a few of my dresses. Attending a social function did not sound appealing. I wished to settle into my new routine and do a bit of quiet exploring with my cousin.

"Adelia, please!" She pleaded. "The couple hosting are good friends of ours, and she was looking forward to meeting you. And please let my maidservant Beatrice tend to your dresses, you have had a long journey and must be tired."

"I am perfectly capable of unpacking my own wardrobe cousin but thank you for being so considerate. Maybe I could consider attending the dinner party." I sighed reluctantly. The exuberance of today's journey was beginning to take its toll on me in the form of sheer exhaustion.

Her eyes lit up. "Wonderful, it is settled then! Besides, are you not excited to make new connections and meet people, of the male population perhaps?"

"No, I wish to avoid making acquaintances with young men altogether." I expressed.

"Are you sure Adelia? Not even the young man from the train station earlier? What if you bump into him again?" She wriggled her eyebrows in a teasing way.

"Especially not him!" I exclaimed. "He was a great annoyance."

Helena laughed and shook her head as if she did not believe my words, but I was telling the truth. "All right, well you are going to come whether you enjoy it or not! I will see you at supper in a little bit." She left me alone to finish unpacking.

When I was done, I sat down on my new bed and took a moment to relax. One dinner party. I could do that for my cousins who had welcomed me into their life. Besides, it would probably not even be all that eventful.

Teaching the children was proving to be both equal parts challenging and rewarding. Eleanor was sweet and compliant, but her brother's favorite pastime was to disrupt the classroom or ignore my efforts to teach him at any cost. One afternoon while I was listening to Eleanor reciting the letters of the alphabet, Alfred dropped his textbooks over the arm of the couch to disturb our lesson.

"Alfred please do not do that." I asked. "Eleanor, you may continue."

"That is A, B, C" She started and then groaned as we heard another thud.

"Just ignore him." I whispered to her. "Good, and which is that one?" I pointed to a letter in the book.

"D, that is E, F." She continued as I saw Alfred watching us from across the room, bemused that I did not acknowledge his behavior. After Eleanor finished, I walked over to him.

"I see you are not interested in reading." I glanced at the books scattered on the floor. "You need to pick them up, that is not how you treat books."

He huffed and started gathering them. "Reading is boring."

"If reading is not stimulating enough for you, I want you to work on arithmetic. You can continue to practice adding and subtracting." I started to tally math problems on a slate. His eyes widened as he realized I was serious.

"No, actually I will try this one. I will at least look at the pictures." Alfred mumbled as he sat back down with a small geography book. I nodded and went back to check on Eleanor, another classroom crisis averted.

Later, Helena poked her head in as I was picking up the classroom at the end of the day.

"How was class?" She asked.

"Eleanor is doing well and will be fully reading soon." I smiled, proud of her progress.

"And what about my little terror of a son, Alfred?"

"He seems to be testing me out still. I have been choosing to ignore some of his misbehavior, which greatly surprised him." I explained.

"Good! That is one thing he loves, getting a reaction out of adults." Helena laughed. "I knew you would get along well with them." I nodded and rearranged a few volumes on the bookshelf.

"So, are you excited for tonight?" Helena asked.

"Oh, the evening dinner party. That is tonight." I had forgotten that I had agreed to attend.

"What are you going to wear?" She asked the essential question that every lady usually ponders before a dining engagement.

I shrugged. "I have not thought about it."

"Would you like some new dresses? We will have to go shopping soon." She stood deep in thought. "I think I might have something you can wear tonight. Follow me." Helena brought me up to her wardrobe and started combing through a rack full of thick colorful fabrics. She selected two dresses, one a rich purple, the other a shimmering silver. "I have not worn these outfits yet. You can have them if you want. The purple would look splendid on you with your hair and eyes."

I picked them up delicately. "Are you sure? I would not want to impose on your generosity."

"Yes! Take them, I already have more than enough dresses. I must admit I love buying new outfits." She confessed and shut her wardrobe swiftly.

"Thank you, Helena. You are too kind."

"Nonsense! I enjoy being in your company and spoiling you a little bit! You are like a younger sister to me. Now, go ahead and get ready for the evening. We will leave by eight."

I walked up the stairs to my room, feeling grateful to have a new option for clothing. I did not want to have to wear the lavender dress I wore to Edith's wedding since heartache and disappointment seemed to be weaved through the fabric, a constant reminder of the past few months.

I dressed and arranged my hair. I did choose to wear the purple gown, with the pleated bodice and fancy ruffled skirt. I put on my mother's pearl necklace and spritzed myself with a dainty perfume that Helena had also gifted me.

While we were driving, I reminded myself of the promise I had made when I left Hastings. I was not going to attach my heart or feelings to any random attractive man that I might meet in London. I was going to focus on myself at present. At peace with that decision, I put on a cheerful face, telling myself that if I could successfully navigate through the next few hours, a restful night's sleep in my well-appointed bed chamber would be my reward.

We entered the house, and I realized that the London definition of an informal dinner party was much different than what I was accustomed to in Hastings. There were a significant number of people mingling and talking in groups. Helena led me over to her friend who was hosting.

"Lilian, this is my cousin Adelia. Adelia this is my good friend Mrs. Lilian Thorne."

"Thank you for inviting me tonight. You live in a lovely house." I acknowledged with a smile.

"It was no trouble at all! I am so glad to meet you. How are you adjusting to London?" Lilian asked. I answered her vaguely and the conversation tittered on for a little while. "Enjoy mingling. And I will see you ladies at the meal." Lilian concluded with a hostess smile and left to speak with her other guests.

"Here are a few people I can introduce you to." Helena grabbed my hand and proceeded to drag me through meetings with several other couples and a few unattached ladies, who took the opportunity to make me feel less than welcome by greeting me with cold civility and false smiles. It seemed they had the determined instinct to view me as competition immediately. As soon as that assumption crossed my mind, I chided myself. Had I turned completely cynical when it came to my peers? I was beginning to question my resilience when I was finally introduced to a young lady who was most gracious on first impression.

"It is nice to meet you, Miss Hadlee. I am Charlotte Castelow." Charlotte was exotically beautiful with raven black hair, round dark eyes, and tan tinted smooth skin. "How are you enjoying London so far?"

"It has been exciting." I replied.

"And you said you were from Hastings?"

"Yes, that is right."

"What is your Hastings like? I have not been to many of England's coastal towns, so I am curious."

"It is nice, and I do enjoy the coast very much, but it can feel small at times. I do believe I have met more people here tonight than I may have in all my years living in Hastings."

She laughed. "Speaking of that you must meet my older brother. He was right here a moment ago." She looked around swiftly and her eyes lit up. "There he is. Nayan!" She beckoned someone over.

"Nayan?" The name sounded foreign, and I could not help but wonder aloud.

"Oh, that is a name my family calls him. My brother's British first name is Edwin." Charlotte explained.

I froze when I heard her say that name. The man at the train station. His name had been Edwin. Surely, this was a ridiculous coincidence. I plastered on a smile, as I turned toward her brother. I looked up and was met with a familiar pair of twinkling sapphire eyes. I do believe my smile faded entirely in that quick moment and my mind went completely blank.

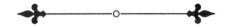

Chapter 8

"**A**h! The lady with no name. What are the chances that we would meet again?" It was now Edwin Castelow's turn to act smug and amused at the current situation.

"You two have met before?" Charlotte was confused.

"Yes, at the train station a couple of weeks ago." He explained before I could speak. "I stepped in when she was in danger of falling. You were quite contentious when we spoke by the way." He looked over at me and then back to his sister. "And she refused to give me her name. I have to say that was a first for me."

"I cannot blame you for not wanting to give your name to a complete and total stranger." Charlotte reassured me and gave her brother a teasing glance.

"Thank you." I told her. I was already beginning to like Charlotte very much.

Of course, my cousin decided to poke her head in at this moment. "Hello, Castelow's. How are you this evening?" She greeted.

"Very well indeed. We are becoming acquainted with your cousin, whom I actually met a while ago at the train station." Edwin stated purposely.

"Oh, Mr. Castelow was the stranger at the train station whom you told me about? What a coincidence." Helena seemed thrilled to have figured out that conundrum. Edwin Castelow looked at me, greatly amused. How grand, now he believed I had talked about him at length to Helena. I desperately wished to become invisible.

Mr. Castelow, seeming completely pleased with himself, addressed me again. "Can we be formally introduced now? I am Mr. Edwin Castelow. And you are?"

"Miss Adelia Hadlee." I conceded.

His eyes widened. "What is your first name?" He asked again, more urgently this time.

"It is impertinent to ask a lady to repeat what she has already told you. It shows that you were not listening the first time, Mr. Castelow." He silently stared back at me, and I grew uncomfortable. I remembered that sometimes men assume that your quips are an attempt to flirt with them. I was not flirting with him. "Adelia. My first name is Adelia." I articulated.

Edwin Castelow seemed to be turning something over in his mind. "A most unusual name." He responded distractedly.

I did not know what to say in response and I chose to disregard his cryptic comment. I focused back on Charlotte. "How old are you Charlotte, if you do not mind me asking?"

"I am eighteen." She answered and then noticed that her older brother was still hovering over us. "Edwin, surely you could find someone else to converse with now?"

"Fine, I will leave you bahan. Miss Hadlee." He bowed and I was obliged to curtsy.

"What did he call you?" I asked after he was completely out of range of hearing me.

"Bahan means sister in Hindi. You see, our mother is from India." Charlotte explained. "We are bilingual."

That made so much sense, as both Charlotte and Edwin were unique in contrast to everyone else. Their dark hair and tan complexions clearly signified they had foreign heritage.

"Do you have Hindi names as well? You called your brother Nayan earlier."

"Yes, that is his Hindi name, Nayan, and my Hindi name is Amaya."

"That is interesting! Tell me about India. How often do you visit?" I thought it amazing that she had heritage from such a faraway land.

Charlotte proceeded to converse with me about details from her most recent trip to India. She explained her father to be a British gentleman who owned a profitable trade business that had ties in India. We continued speaking with one another until it was time for the meal. I then followed Helena to our assigned seating where I was able to peacefully eat and only be present every so often in the conversation around the table.

It grew more tiresome after the meal, trying to blend in with the wealth and aristocracy. It was almost as if I was an understudy in a play and I did not know my lines. I snuck away at one point and sat down on a quiet bench next to a doorway, leading to a room that was filled with guests milling about, engaged in friendly chatter. I was rubbing my temples, trying to get rid of an impending headache, when I heard the voices of young men talking boisterously together, one of them being Edwin Castelow.

"Edwin! Did you not say you met a brash young lady at the train station recently?" One of them named Michael spoke.

"Yes, I did help a young woman the other day, she was traveling alone you see, and needed assistance. She refused to acknowledge me and did not seem to appreciate my help. She was most disagreeable."

My blood began to boil. That is not what happened at all! I distinctively remember thanking him for helping me, and then he refused to leave me alone.

"Oh Edwin, come now. It sounds as if she refused to flatter you, is that why you were irritated? Was she a beauty?" Another man, James teased.

"Her looks were tempting enough, but her lack of decorum and uneven temperament were enough to detract from her beauty."

"It certainly seems that this young woman has unsettled you, Edwin." James sounded amused at his friend's words.

Edwin continued, haughty as ever. "In all seriousness, my point is that if a gentleman takes the time to assist, the lady should feel obliged to display gratitude and respect towards him."

I cursed my extremely sensitive ears, as I have an exceptional talent for overhearing conversations that I am sometimes the subject of, but not actively a part of. I stood up quickly and breathed out a sigh of annoyance as I mulled over his words. Edwin no doubt viewed himself as a high authority, presuming that all young women should gaze at him with admiration and stroke his ego. In my opinion, a gentleman should not force a lady to engage in conversation, and what did I know of him that he deserved my immediate respect? There was no chance of him earning my respect now. How I desperately wanted to storm the room and say those things to his face! After a moment of contemplation, I realized my strategy to avoid young Alfred's actions would work just as well for dealing with Edwin Castelow.

Still seething, I tried to appear calm as Charlotte appeared and we continued our conversation. I honestly wondered how two siblings could be so different, one meek and mild, the other so arrogant.

It finally came time to take our leave, and Charlotte insisted on walking out with me to my cousins' carriage. When I saw Edwin follow his sister right behind us, my walk and energy were charged with an emotion of resentment at what I had overheard him say earlier. I bid Charlotte goodbye and waited as Cousin Theodore helped Cousin Helena into the coach. As I realized that Theodore could not assist me into our carriage since he was trapped under Helena's petticoats against the seat, it became apparent that Edwin was waiting to assist me up. When a friend of Edwin's distracted him by saying goodnight, I seized the opportunity to slip past him and nimbly situated myself into the carriage without assistance. A few seconds later, Edwin turned back around and noticed, to his surprise, that I was already seated in place, smoothing out my skirt.

"Miss Hadlee, I would have offered to assist you." Edwin explained and smiled at me.

"Oh no, Mr. Castelow. I would not presume to inflict my 'uneven temperament and disagreeable self' upon you by asking for assistance." I tersely replied.

Edwin blinked reticently, his lower jaw dropping slightly as he stood there aghast, still processing my words. I took an inordinate amount of satisfaction in watching Edwin Castelow's smile disappear as he realized I had repeated, word for word, his biased opinion of me that he expressed earlier to a private audience. I had to suppress my laughter as we traveled off for home.

"Why did you say that to Mr. Castelow?" Helena asked me.

"Because he insulted me with those exact words." I proceeded to tell her about what I overheard.

"What a shame he said something unpleasant about you, he does not seem to act like that typically, especially in front of available ladies. You know there is a lengthy list of young women who would gladly fall at the feet of Edwin Castelow to make him their hero." Helena joked playfully.

"I can assure you my name need not be on that list." I responded. "Besides, this supposed hero has now tainted himself in my view with his thoughtless remarks."

The next couple of weeks passed quickly as I was kept busy with teaching my students. Eleanor was now reading and both children were taking an interest in the educational curriculum. London was experiencing exceptional weather for the autumn season. Accordingly, Helena and I took advantage of the sunshine by planning nature excursions at the public park across the street. Alfred was impressed when I told him what I had arranged for the day and informed me that his previous governess had never encouraged such expeditions. I was pleased that he finally agreed to show civility towards me and had grown more excited about learning with each passing week.

As we sojourned over to the park, we took some time to observe the whirling, twirling leaves that danced off of their branches into the autumn wind. The children received a brief science lesson on how the pigment in leaves decreases, which causes the leaves to drop and spin from the trees. They took great pleasure in jumping onto the piles of leaves and chasing each other on the green grass. I laughed heartedly as I observed the two siblings getting along and having fun together. I was playing with the children when I heard my name being called in the distance.

"Hello, Adelia!" Charlotte Castelow greeted me. I turned and saw that she was standing with an older woman and, to my instant displeasure, her older brother.

"Hello, Charlotte. It is nice to see you."

"This is my mother, Bimala. Mama this is my new friend Miss Hadlee." Charlotte introduced me to her mother, and I said hello. "And of course, you have already met Edwin."

"Miss Hadlee." Edwin acknowledged. I barely responded with an obliged curtsy.

"We decided to come for a walk after attending to a few errands in town." Charlotte explained their presence in the park, and I nodded in acknowledgement.

"Charlotte tells me you two have become good friends." Mrs. Castelow addressed me. "Are you enjoying your time in London?"

We continued to talk for a few minutes and Mrs. Castelow asked me about my teaching of the children. She seemed a most calm and wise lady and what I observed of her temperament reminded me of her daughter Charlotte. She had the same dark hair as her children, now streaked with silver strands and a warm smile. Thankfully, Edwin stayed silent, and I did not have to engage with him at all. Throughout this time Alfred and Eleanor had still been playing but they suddenly rushed up to me as I was talking.

"Adelia, look! I found another leaf that is not broken!" Alfred exclaimed, proud of himself.

"I found that!" Eleanor complained, upset at her brother taking credit for her accomplishment.

"Did Eleanor actually find that leaf, Alfred?" I asked trying to be judicious.

"Yes." He responded quietly.

"What should you do for your sister then?" I reasoned.

"Give it back to her." He answered and gingerly handed it back to his little sister.

"Thank you." She responded and clutched to my skirts shyly.

"Yes, thank you. We can find you more leaves to take home for yourself." I told him.

"And then we can press them in a book like you promised!" Alfred reminded me with excitement.

"Yes, we can do that." I responded with a laugh and turned back towards the Castelow's. Charlotte and her mother were discussing something with each other, but I was completely unaware that Edwin had been quietly observing me interact with the children and was now looking at me with smiling eyes as an unrecognizable expression swept across his face. Amusement perhaps? I quickly dismissed it from my mind and turned back to Charlotte.

"I am so glad we ran into you today!" Charlotte told me. "I was just telling Mama how much I would enjoy inviting you to tea."

"Yes that would be nice, and I was very glad to meet you Mrs. Castelow." I smiled and bid them goodbye.

"We will send an invitation for tea soon." Charlotte smiled happily and waved as they walked away.

"Come children, let us get ready to go." I held Eleanor's hand and I directed them to gather up their things. I felt as if someone was looking at me or watching us and I discreetly turned while busying myself with helping Eleanor. I saw the Castelow's a few paces ahead, Charlotte and her mother talking, but Edwin was still observing the three of us and more noticeably looking over at me. He swiftly turned his head the moment I turned my gaze toward his direction. When we were ready to leave a few moments later, I was relieved to see that the Castelow's had moved along farther into the park, and I walked home with the children.

After we returned home, I spent some time in my room before supper. Why was Edwin Castelow's behavior so vexing to me? Never mind. I realized how refreshing it felt to not be distressed over a young man's actions, and I still remembered how liberating it was to call Edwin out on his ill-mannered behavior on the evening of the gathering. Besides, I wanted to focus on my new friend Charlotte. It was refreshing to be around a young lady who was modest and graceful in a natural way. Yes, tea with Charlotte and Mrs. Castelow would be a delight!

It was a chilly Saturday that Charlotte had chosen to invite me to afternoon tea. I bundled up in my favorite wrap and coat and set out, giving the cab driver the address that was listed on my invitation. The Castelow's estate was located a few minutes outside of the busy section of London. A sharp turn down a long-graveled driveway revealed a tall and imposing house with greenery and multiple gardens sprawled out behind it. Several chimneys and sharp peaks in the roof seemed to contribute to the stature of the home. The front of the house had a sweeping porch with a well-defined line of steps leading up to the front door. I walked up gingerly and was shown into the main foyer by a quiet maidservant. She brought me up to a cheerful parlor on the West side of the house where I found Charlotte and her mother waiting for me. We went through the usual traditional greetings and then sat down to afternoon tea. After an hour or so of discussion on various topics and aspects of life, Charlotte asked if I would enjoy a tour of the gardens outside.

"I know the plants are not in bloom this time of year, but I do delight in taking walks out in the fresh air!" Charlotte explained.

"That would be wonderful, I also enjoy the exercise." I agreed. I said goodbye to Mrs. Castelow, and Charlotte and I traversed down the staircase, chatting all the way. We both looked up as we heard her mother call down from the balcony.

"Charlotte, my ladki, do not forget your coat along with a wrap for your neck! I would not want you catching cold." Mrs. Castelow walked away after reminding her daughter.

"She worries about me since I do have trouble staying healthy in the wintertime." Charlotte told me. "Let me go get my coat, and where did I leave my wrap? Mary?" Charlotte called for her lady's maid and went back up the stairs. "I will be right back Adelia!"

Charlotte's absence left me awkwardly standing at the bottom of the Castelow's staircase waiting for her to return. As I donned my coat I observantly looked around and noticed a long hallway to the right of the staircase lined with doors. I heard men's voices speaking behind one of them and then the door opened. Out walked Edwin, heading right towards my direction, which made me instinctively want to tuck myself away out of view. Why did I unfortunately have to keep running into him? Why did I feel the need to conceal myself?

I was in his environment, his family home nonetheless, I reminded myself. He had now noticed me.

"Miss Hadlee. This is a surprise." Edwin walked over to my proximity.

"I am waiting for your sister Charlotte; she is going to show me the gardens." I justified my reason for standing in his family's house all by myself.

"Yes, that is right, you were invited to tea." He remembered his sister's plans. "And how are you doing today?"

What was taking Charlotte so long to find her garments? "I am well." I answered civilly. I now stayed quiet as I worked on wrapping my scarf around my neck.

After a moment of observing my silence and standoffish demeanor, Edwin spoke. "You know Miss Hadlee, I get the feeling that you do not like me very much."

"Honestly, I thought it was you yourself that did not care for my temperament at all." I said with tempered indignation and a pointed look in his direction.

"If you are referring to something that you overheard one night while eavesdropping, I must say do not take it too seriously. It was unreasonable frustration on my part, and I am now starting to regret my words." He explained. "Can we put this behind us and perhaps work towards becoming friends?" He reached out his hand into the space between us, expecting me to return the gesture.

I had not yet put on my gloves for going outside, and I really did not want to touch his hand with my bare hand. Apparently, my few seconds of contemplation were too long for Edwin because his countenance darkened, and he sharply withdrew his hand that he had just offered a moment ago.

"Glad to see you are warming up to the idea." Edwin spoke with an edge of bitterness. "And a good day to you as well Miss Hadlee."

Charlotte finally rushed down the stairs right after Edwin had spoken these words. "I am all ready to go out Adelia! Oh, hello Edwin! Where are you going?" We both watched as he stalked over towards an exit.

"I am going out." He answered gruffly and then he was gone.

Charlotte looked over at me carefully. "I am sorry I kept you waiting. Did Edwin speak to you at all? He seemed to be in a bad mood, so you will have to forgive his impoliteness."

"Do not apologize for that." I told her as we walked out in the crisp air and beaming sunlight. "I did not come to converse with your older brother. I came to spend time with you, Charlotte, as your friend. We are friends, right?" I smiled at her.

She seemed happy and smiled back at me. "Yes, we are!"

On the subject of friends, I finally received a letter from Edith a couple of days after I had tea with Charlotte. It was obvious that she was absorbed and preoccupied with her married life. I was greatly irritated by the final paragraph of her letter that read as follows.

"But I do miss seeing you, Adelia! It seems very dull around here as we are now going into winter, and our annual family dinners are really the only source of general amusement. I have been meaning to say that I am sorry for you that it did not work out with Henry, but there are other suitable young men that you and I know of. I am sure they would love to get to know you better! Write to me about London and then you must hurry back to Hastings soon!"

Your friend,

Edith Ansley.

I set the letter down and started unpinning my hair as I had now retired to my room for the evening. I breathed out a sigh of annoyance since Edith was assuming I was already over and done with my feelings for Oliver's brother and ready to move on with a new suiter. Perhaps I was not interested in meeting someone or courting right now! I decided Edith really could not presume sympathy for me because she married the Ansley man whom she had been desperately in love with for so many months.

Picking up the current novel I was reading, I focused on absorbing myself into the pages in order to avoid painful memories that were alarmingly trying to creep back into my mind. It worked and I soon lost track of time as I became transfixed by the words on the paper. When I finally came to a stopping point in the plot of the story, I saw that my candle was burned down, and the clock read close to midnight.

As I pulled back my covers to get into bed, I heard an urgent knock on my door. I cautiously opened it to see Helena, who had obviously trekked up the stairs in a hastened motion.

"Adelia! I am sorry to disrupt you but something peculiar has happened! Charlotte Castelow's lady's maid, Mary, is here and says she desperately needs to talk to you!" Helena blurted out her reason for rousing me at this late hour. I looked over her shoulder to see that she had brought Mary up with her.

"Is anything serious the matter?" I asked Mary, growing fearful.

Mary's eyes had grown huge and pleading. "It is Miss Charlotte! She has fallen terribly ill this evening and I do not know what to do!"

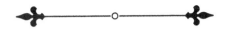

Chapter 9

Helena and Mary had now pushed through the bedroom door. "What kind of illness?" I asked while I mentally thought out what remedies would be needed and pulled on a dress over my chemise.

"We are not sure, she is having trouble breathing for one thing, and she appears to be feverish!"

"Has the family Doctor been sent for?" Helena inquired.

"Yes, but we received a message back saying he will not be available for a few hours since he was called away across town to help a mother delivering a child." Mary updated me on the circumstances. "Mr. and Mrs. Castelow are away from London right now, and we are all very concerned, but Charlotte asked for Miss Adelia specifically."

"Take me to her then, please!" I requested, grabbing my apothecary bag. "I might be able to help her until the Doctor comes."

We all hurriedly walked down the stairs. "I will probably stay with her into the night, you should most likely not expect me home until morning." I informed Helena right before I left.

"Of course!" Helena waved me off with an anxious smile. "I hope Charlotte pulls through!"

It was an uneasy drive to the Castelow's as I was concerned about the true state of my friend's wellbeing. It started to rain heavily, and the coach splashed and jostled through puddles and muck. We navigated the driveway of the Castelow estate, disembarked from the coach, and proceeded to make our way up to the front door. Mary led me up the stairs and we turned down several corridors to reach Charlotte's bedroom. The first thing I noticed was Charlotte lying in her bed, but then my eyes darted over to see the shadow of Edwin sitting near his sister. His eyes were downcast, and his hand was cradling his forehead. I heard him sigh forlornly, and then he became aware of my presence as I swiftly walked over to the other side of Charlotte.

"Miss Hadlee!" Edwin stood up.

"How is Charlotte doing?" I asked matter-of-factly.

"Not well, I do not understand why she fell ill so suddenly, she seemed fine earlier." He was now wringing his hands nervously. "Charlotte asked for you a little bit ago when she was still coherent. She said you would know what to do. I am puzzled by her statement, what did she mean?"

I recalled my conversation with her the other day during tea. "We have discussed some of my experience assisting my aunt. I was taught how to care for sick ones and heal with apothecary remedies." I quickly explained as I assessed Charlotte's appearance. She was breathing raggedly, and beads of sweat had formed across her feverish forehead.

"Adelia." I heard Charlotte whisper through parched lips. She had recognized me, but she appeared listless, and I knew it was only a passing moment as she slipped in and out of consciousness.

"Hello, Charlotte." I uttered soothingly. "We are going to get you feeling better, just rest for now." I turned back to Edwin. "She definitely has a fever; we have to cool her down immediately."

"She looks so helpless!" Edwin moaned and started to pace the room. He was dismayed over his sister's condition, and I paused for a moment to take in the unfamiliar disheveled appearance of Edwin Castelow. His dark hair was mussed, clothes crumpled, and dark circles were starting to form under his eyes. He was radiating tense energy, but before it had a chance to affect me, I recalled helping Emer Moore last summer and what my aunt had told me.

"The most important thing about taking care of a person in distress is to stay levelheaded and keep your focus on the patient."

"We have to stay calm." I addressed Edwin and he snapped back to attention. "Charlotte needs a peaceful environment to rest. You will have to listen to me if I direct you to do something. If we work together, we can help your sister."

"Of course, anything. What should I do?"

"We need to elevate her in order to open up her airways. Can you help me prop her up on these pillows?" After he assisted me in repositioning Charlotte, I got to work on mixing an elixir for my patient to ingest. Edwin came back into the room carrying a few supplies that I had sent him to fetch.

"Here are the linens you asked for." He noticed me measuring out liquids. "What are you going to give her?" His question had a protective, non-aggressive tone and I realized as an older brother he was routinely used to safeguarding his younger sister.

"Elderberry syrup, to start with. I have been given this myself and I have administered it to others several times before. It should help reduce the fever and inflammatory response." I reassured him and he nodded while watching me help his sister. I rubbed diluted peppermint oil onto her forehead and neck to hopefully lessen any aching symptoms and help diminish the swollen lymph nodes that had formed under the skin surrounding Charlotte's neck and behind her ears. I asked Mary to bring up cooled tea water, and I mixed up a soothing chamomile drink so we could try to hydrate Charlotte. Edwin accommodated my requests as we cooperated and took care of her side by side.

For the first few hours, Charlotte's condition did not improve much, and I tried my best to make her comfortable and maintain the dosage of medicinal elderberry syrup. The adrenaline of caretaking gave me the energy to stay ever vigilant by my friend's side. There was a terrifying moment in the early morning hours when Charlotte became unresponsive and had gone mostly limp while lying on her bed. I was became anxious, but I hid my uneasiness from Edwin, as his emotional state became somewhat fragile from worrying and being attentive to his sick sister.

"Amaya." Edwin spoke softly, calling Charlotte by her familiar name. "Stay with me. Please." I saw him take her hand and squeeze it gently. The raw emotion I heard in his pleading voice made me feel an immense measure of compassion for Edwin in his anguish for his sister. He looked at me with elation when Charlotte grasped his hand in response to his words. I smiled back in relief, and thankfully, Charlotte's condition improved greatly from that moment forward.

A little bit later, after evaluating Charlotte's breathing, I left the room to go find Mary to ask for more linens. I almost ran into Edwin, who was reentering from taking leave for sustenance.

"How is Charlotte now?" Edwin inquired.

"I believe she is doing much better. Her fever has broken, and I think the oils have palliated her breathing." In that moment, the gravity of the evening's events began to rush through my mind, and the exhaustion from caregiving caught up to me. The hallway started to spin, and feeling faint, I slightly stumbled forward.

"Miss Hadlee, are you alright?" Edwin steadied me with his hands and was peering into my face, trying to determine what was wrong.

"I feel tired, that is all." I looked up at him and saw how close in proximity we were to each other. Edwin was still wearing his wrinkled sleep clothes, no doubt because he had been called out of bed earlier to attend to his sister. For a brief moment, my eyes settled on his exposed collarbone that was protruding from beneath his white shirt collar and I recognized how irregular it was for me to see him in these circumstances. I let go of his arm in the next instant when I became aware that I was still holding onto it for support.

"You really must stop falling into my arms, Miss Hadlee." Edwin teased me, and despite myself, I felt a smile tug at my lips.

"I am fine!" I shook my head. "I must insist you refrain from jesting, Mr. Castelow, it is getting tiresome."

Gazing directly into my tired eyes, Edwin smiled softly. Once again, I recognized the same noticeable expression in his glimmering eyes that I had observed at the park a few weeks prior. Feeling self-conscious, I deliberately broke our eye contact with a slight turn of my head.

"Would you like something to eat or drink? You must be hungry; you have been tending to Charlotte most of the night." He asked me, but it was not really a question as he started to direct me down the hallway to where Mary was. "Mary, please get a cup of tea and some food for Miss Adelia to eat. I will sit with Charlotte until you come back to her room."

Edwin had been right; I was famished, so I sat quietly and enjoyed my sustenance. I could not help comparing my interactions with him during the night to how briskly he had spoken the other day when he had grown impatient with me. Edwin's temperament was now altered, and his speech was very gentle. I reasoned that we had just pulled his sister through a terrible state of illness, so understandably he was feeling relief from that.

When I went back up to the room, I re-examined Charlotte and administered one last dose of elderberry syrup. I was numbly tired, my legs and arms were aching, complaining at me for staying awake all night. The rush of adrenaline from keeping vigil over Charlotte was now wearing off, and I began to experience the full effects of sleep deprivation.

"Charlotte does seem to be much improved. You should rest if you are really tired." Edwin suggested after noticing my repeated yawns and heavy blinking eyelids.

I hesitantly sat down on the divan across the room that was near Charlotte's bed. Yes, this felt heavenly. I told myself I would rest for only a few moments as I closed my eyes. The next thing I knew, I awoke to a new voice in the room. The Doctor had finally come, and the purple light filtering in through the windows indicated it was near sunrise. I sat up, not wanting to remove myself from my snug spot. I then crinkled my brow in confusion as I did not remember putting a blanket on myself when I had sat down to rest. I glanced over at Edwin and saw that he was talking to the Doctor. I delicately removed the blanket and walked over to where they were standing.

"Is this Miss Hadlee?" The Doctor addressed me when I came into his view.

"Yes." I answered.

"You took good care of Charlotte. I am impressed by your healing skills Miss Hadlee." He praised me and then turned back to Edwin. "And I am not trying to be morbid, but I think it is important for you both to know that if Miss Hadlee had not been here to help your sister, Charlotte may not have come through the fever."

I swallowed when we heard those grim words and Edwin looked over at me with a somber expression. I think we were both contemplating how the night could have gone if Charlotte had not responded to my care. Edwin seemed on the verge of saying something else to me, but the Doctor called him over to finish their conversation about further instructions for his sister. I walked over to the bedstand and gathered up the medicinal supplies and returned them to my apothecary bag.

"Goodbye, my friend. I will see you soon." I murmured to Charlotte who still lay peacefully asleep. I slipped out of the room quietly without anyone else noticing and told Mary I was ready to leave. I was put in a coach, and I made it back home in what seemed like a matter of minutes. The servants at the house let me in and I asked the housekeeper to tell Helena I had arrived home and was going back to bed. My head was still swarming with details, processing everything that had happened, but I slipped into bed and fell asleep immediately.

When I finally awoke, I found out that I had slept nearly into the next morning. Still groggily half-awake, the events of the night before replayed in my mind, and I gently rubbed my eyes to awaken myself further. Peacefulness settled on me when I remembered that Charlotte had been doing better when I left her. I resolved to pay her a visit after she had enough time to recuperate.

After missing a day of instruction with Alfred and Eleanor, I was glad to return to my routine of teaching. Their happy faces and animated personalities seemed to brighten up the house throughout the next few days of London rain. One of those tedious afternoons, after lessons had finished for the day, I was sitting with Helena in the parlor. Helena got up to see who rang the doorbell at one point, right after the mail had been delivered. I stayed in the room and picked up an envelope addressed to me from Aunt Leah. I sat back down, eager to read what she had written.

November 16th, 1857

Dear Adelia,

How have you been my dear sweet girl? Your last letter found us well, although we do continuously miss you. I had to pen you a quick correspondence, for we have had an interesting scenario arise. A solicitor contacted us yesterday wishing to communicate with you, thinking you were currently residing at our address. Something has come up regarding your late father's legacy that needs settling, but the solicitor needs to speak to you directly as you are now twenty-one. Richard and I wish to come visit, in order to see you of course, but also to be there in the event you may need assistance addressing these business matters. Write back to let me know if our proposition will sit well with your plans and hopefully we will see you soon. Please do not be too worried about this news, as it is probably nothing to be concerned about and we can discuss further details in person. Give our love to Helena, Theodore, and the children.

Your Loving Aunt,

Leah Hadlee.

Her words confused me, to say the least. Since I had lived with my aunt and uncle most of my life, I had always presumed there had not been much of an estate to settle after my father's death. In knowing my tendency to fret or overthink matters, my aunt had advised me to not be overly concerned, but I did not listen. I ruminated on the hazy memories I had with my father; the last time having seen him being when I was a small girl. I was lost in my thoughts, wishing I possessed the key to unlocking what this all meant when I heard footsteps make their way into the room.

I stood up, still staring at my letter. "Helena, the letter was somewhat vague, I have to ask you if…" I started to speak to Helena, but I then stifled a gasp when I saw that it was not my cousin, but rather Edwin Castelow standing before me.

"Hello." Edwin spoke. "Do you need to see Mrs. Braxton? I can wait to speak with you, if so."

I let my right hand containing the letter settle alongside the skirt of my dress and centered my focus on him. "No, it can keep. Is Charlotte alright?" I asked with an urgent breath and wide eyes.

"Yes." He reassured me. "Charlotte is doing much better and seems to be recovering quickly."

My anxiety melted away when I heard that good news. "I am glad to hear that. I have been planning to visit her once she has regained her strength and will be better able to receive a visitor."

"I came to see you." Edwin furrowed his brow as he searched for the right words. I noticed minuscule drops of rain from the light mist outside glinting throughout the waves of his dark hair. "I came to speak with you that is. I did not get an opportunity yet to properly express my gratitude for your willingness to come and care for my sister the other night. It was a most selfless and courageous act and we both know you saved Charlotte's life."

"It was my honor and privilege to provide assistance as Charlotte's friend, you need not exaggerate my actions. I am sincerely happy that she is feeling better."

"You and I heard what the Doctor said regarding the effect of your care on Charlotte's health. I do not believe I have ever witnessed a young woman act as you did during such a dire situation. You have skills and abilities that are rarely seen amongst the general populace of young ladies."

"I was acting purely on instinct and applying what I have learned to do over the years." I felt that he was giving me excessive praise for my actions. "Besides, I am surely not a singular young lady that has the ability to rise to the occasion. Women by nature are quite capable creatures." I arched my brow, waiting for his rebuttal.

"You most certainly have demonstrated that fact for me."

I had been expecting him to bristle at my eagerness to challenge his words. Instead, he easily seemed to agree with my point of view.

"I wished to address you that morning, but when I looked for you, I was informed you had left." He continued speaking of when he had seen me last.

"I was extremely tired, and I left quietly." I answered simply.

"Well, I would have escorted you home if you had wished." Edwin told me, leaning in closer, voice dropping gently. "I must ask, did I do something that would have influenced you to want to take leave so suddenly?"

"No, you did not. My work was done, and I determined it was best to remove myself from the situation at that point."

Edwin nodded and his expression softened. "I was unsure of myself because as you know I have been guilty of making foolish remarks or becoming abrupt with others." He shook his head with a wry smile, seemingly hinting at our previous interactions with each other. "The circumstances were demanding that night, and afterward I could scarcely remember the conversations that had passed between us."

"We seemed to get along just fine when we were both concerned about Charlotte." I then turned towards a desk by the window and set my letter down. Edwin continued to try and carry on a friendly conversation in the following few minutes. I endeavored to listen to him, but my mind kept drifting back to the puzzling letter I had received from my aunt.

"You seem a little distracted at the moment. Is everything alright?" Edwin asked after I had barely answered a question that he had posed. His unbreaking eye contact and slightly tilted head told me he was focused and interested in knowing what was troubling me.

"It is nothing too alarming, hopefully. I received a letter from my aunt informing me of a family business matter that will personally involve me. I am trying to make sense of it all, it is very perplexing."

Edwin listened and was quiet for a moment. "I have taken up enough of your time this afternoon. I will take my leave for you to be able to discuss things with your family."

I was grateful that he had not pressed me for further details regarding my circumstances. "Thank you Mr. Castelow."

"Please, call me Edwin. We spent a whole night together caring for my sister, I was hoping we could be on a first-name basis now."

"Alright, Edwin." I agreed to his wishes, which resulted in a broad smile bestowed upon me.

"Adelia." He said as we moved toward the door. "Please let me know if there is anything I can do to assist you in the future with your family situation. I am at your service."

"Thank you, I will keep your offer in mind Edwin." I smiled with appreciation, and he stepped out into the hallway.

"Goodbye, Adelia."

"Goodbye."

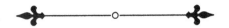

Chapter 10

"What exactly was in the letter that made it critical for Uncle Richard and you to come and see me in person?" I investigated the mysterious situation as I sat with my aunt and uncle. They had arrived in town earlier that morning and we were now visiting in my cousin's drawing-room. Helena and Theodore were out at the moment, but we would all be dining together later.

"The letter did not state much of anything else other than what I told you in our correspondence." My Aunt Leah handed me the small paper. I reached over to grasp the solicitor's letter and glanced over it hurriedly. She was right, the solicitor had not given us much detail.

"The solicitor, Mr. Wilson, handled your father's business endeavors, and claims that the meeting between us needs to be handled in person." Uncle Richard explained. "Since Mr. Wilson is located in London, it is more efficient to come here for conducting business affairs."

"And now that you are here, you have contacted Mr. Wilson again to arrange an appointment?" I asked.

"Yes, we will meet with him in a couple of days." Aunt Leah informed me.

"I cannot imagine what he will have to discuss with me regarding my father. It does not make any sense."

"Sometimes things arise years after a death, details that were missed or not handled correctly. We will have to wait and see." Uncle Richard said nonchalantly.

"Let us put that aside for now. Tell me how the last few months have passed. What have you been doing?" My aunt inquired. I smiled and started recounting my comings and goings over the last several months. As we conversed, I realized how much I had missed both my aunt and uncle. They were the embodiment of home and seeing the two of them again made me think of lovely warm memories of Cliffside. Twinges of homesickness swept over me and put me in a wistful mood. I could smell the sweet baked goods and spices that wafted through the kitchen this time of year and I thought of the cozy nights wrapped up snug by a fire. Even though I was feeling nostalgic, it was still exciting to speak of my time in London. My aunt and uncle listened as I regaled them with some of the happenings I had experienced as a tourist in the city and laughed when I spoke of stories about Helena's children. While we were all talking, Alfred and Eleanor poked their heads in through the doorway.

"Come here for a moment." I beckoned them to come closer.

"Adelia!" Eleanor rushed over to me. "You said I could play with your paints today."

"I can help you with that in a minute." I told her and motioned over to my aunt and uncle. "Alfred and Eleanor, this is my aunt and uncle. They have come to visit me for a few days."

After my aunt and uncle talked with the children for a couple of minutes, I relented to Eleanor's begging and stood up to help her. My uncle sat with Alfred, and Aunt Leah followed Eleanor and me over to my painting supplies. I set Eleanor up with my paints, and afterward, I saw Aunt Leah glancing at my open sketchbook.

"Can I look through your sketches?" Aunt Leah asked. I nodded approvingly and she proceeded to leaf through the drawings. "These are excellent." She complimented me as she studied a few sketches that I had completed recently. "They seem happier, more cheerful."

I compared my recent drawings to the ones I had done a few months ago. The new subjects were soft and painted with warm colors which was a sharp contrast to the older black and white sketches that were melancholy.

"I am happy." I told her. "I believe I have regained my cheerful spirit."

Aunt Leah put her arm around me and gave me a warm smile. "That is good. I am glad you are enjoying London."

"Me too."

Later, at supper, we all talked more about my presence in the household and the happenings of the last few weeks. Helena seemed all too eager to enlighten my aunt and uncle on certain details.

"Adelia has been busy, considering she nursed a friend back to life and was called upon by the older brother." Helena teased with a dramatic flair. My aunt and uncle responded simultaneously.

"You helped a sick friend?" Aunt Leah questioned.

"Who is this young man that called on you?" Uncle Richard asked with fatherly protectiveness.

"My new friend Charlotte Castelow fell ill recently while her parents were away. I was asked to come help one night and everything that Aunt Leah has taught me regarding supplementary natural medicine was put to good use." I briefly explained with a grateful glance towards my aunt.

"And what about the older brother calling on you?" My uncle further probed.

"A few days later, her older brother visited me in person as I suppose he felt compelled to thank me for the assistance I provided to his sister." I looked over at my cousin. "It was one visit Helena, one. Oh, and thank you for sending him into the room without warning." I retorted sarcastically. I had been irritated when I realized she had purposely let Edwin in to speak with me without informing me first.

"You are welcome." She smiled. "And was that really all he said? For I thought I overheard him saying as he was leaving that he was willing to help you with anything you needed in the future. Quite the gentleman."

"You were eavesdropping?" I was beginning to understand what an annoying habit that was. "Helena!"

"The door was open; it is hard to not overhear conversations sometimes." Helena shrugged innocently.

"Touché." I said simply. As there was nothing else to say on that topic, the conversation moved to a new subject, but I could tell that my aunt and uncle found this exchange between Helena and I to be most humorous.

The brief mention of the Castelow's reminded me that I needed to call on Charlotte. I sent a note to her the following day asking if I could visit her the next morning. I got an excited approval in response from her. As I got ready that morning, I visited with my aunt.

"I shall not be long. I am briefly checking in with my friend Charlotte and then I will back." I said as I pinned my hat on.

"This is the friend who was sick and also has the older brother?" Aunt Leah confirmed.

"Yes. I do not know why Helena teases me so. When I first came here she acted as if she was determined to have me meet someone and form a connection."

"She is acting like a sister that is all. Older sisters tease." My aunt explained with her prior experience of being an older sister.

"I do not truly mind, but honestly there is nothing to tease me about. I believe Charlotte appreciates that my motives for friendship are sincere." I reflected on previous events. "Besides, even if I was to form an attachment to a young man, I would be determined to not be as silly as last time. One would have to forcefully draw my sentiments out; I would not make it easy for the young man."

"Some discretion is appropriate at times, but you showed yourself to be modest in that situation. You are too critical of yourself Adelia."

"I am certainly glad I had not been more forward in my interactions with the aforementioned person because I saved myself some embarrassment. In conclusion, it was a cautionary tale, and I learned the lesson." I explained while searching for my coat.

"I am happy you have found peace of mind, but I would not wish you to feel that you have to shut off your emotions from a future worthy suiter."

"If it would prevent me from experiencing that amount of pain again, it seems wise to do so." I voiced quietly.

"Try to not be overly concerned about it. That way your feelings or emotions will not instantly get involved if a relationship develops over time. Remember that a natural romance usually blossoms from a strong friendship first. Focus on living your life, and whatever happens, happens. You will know when the right person comes along." My aunt wisely spoke.

I smiled as I assimilated her words. Her advice made perfect sense, as always. "That is what I intend to do. I am focused on developing my inner self and nurturing those who are important to me." I kissed her on the cheek as I got ready to leave the room. "Our appointment is at two o'clock, right?"

"Yes, two o'clock."

"Well, I will be back for dinner and then the appointment!" I said cheerfully.

"Enjoy visiting with your friend Charlotte!" She called as I went down the stairs to get into the coach.

Charlotte was in good health and cheerful spirits when I saw her. The two of us happily chatted away, talking about the events that had transpired.

"My whole family is appreciative that you came, and I am most thankful that you were there to help me."

"I am happy to see that you are feeling better Charlotte." I smiled as she began to say something else.

"I am indebted to you. Now, let me repay you for what you did for me." She smiled, and it seemed to have a mischievous flare to it.

I rushed to dismiss any obligations she supposed I was expecting. "That is not necessary. Your recovery is enough in return for my efforts."

"I have an important piece of information to share with you." Charlotte informed me and then paused. I beckoned her to continue with an anticipatory glance. "I need you to listen carefully as I speak to you and not immediately deny what I tell you." She directed me while I waited in suspense.

"Alright, I will try." I agreed to her terms.

Charlotte sat for a moment, eyes cast upward, contemplating how to begin her important topic. "Did my brother call to speak with you?"

I recalled my brief conversation with Edwin that occurred the previous week. "Yes, he did."

"And what did he say to you?" She was watching me, dark eyes wide and an expectant smile hesitating on her lips.

I was confused by the eager tone of her question. "He told me he was grateful for my coming to assist while you were ill."

"Is that all?"

"Yes." I noticed Charlotte's hopeful expression shift slightly. "Were you wishing for a different answer? When he came to speak with me that day, I had just received a letter from my family. My mind was occupied, and my attention was not solely focused on our conversation."

"Oh, well that must have been it then. He noticed that you were preoccupied."

I could tell that it was Charlotte's mind that was preoccupied now, pondering over a distant subject. "Charlotte what does this topic have to do with you telling me something significant?"

Charlotte seemed to come back to my attention and grabbed my hand lightly with enthusiasm. "My brother would most likely not want me to tell you this, but I am going to speak up as you are my dear friend, and it is in your best interest. Adelia, Edwin holds you in high esteem and is developing a strong affection for you."

Charlotte talked with such animation and a sparkle in her eyes.

"Are you sure you are feeling completely better Charlotte?" I asked with skepticism. "You seem quite exuberant right now."

"I am completely fine." Charlotte reassured me. "Adelia, you said you would listen to me."

I slightly shook my head with my eyes closed. "I know I did. Your statement caught me off guard. Why are you mentioning this to me if you feel that he would not want me to know? Perhaps you are mistaken. From our first meeting, Edwin and I have seemed destined to disagree whenever the opportunity arises."

"Adelia, you do not disagree with him, you challenge him." Charlotte emphasized. "My brother has never met a young lady such as yourself. You are not afraid to stand up to him or speak your mind in his presence. Most of the young women that he has associated with in the past have been all too eager to seek his admiration and show off for him. You carry yourself differently."

I stayed silent, as she had asked me to do, allowing Charlotte's revelation to sink in. She continued on. "And on account of my brother coming across as stern or aloof in his speech or manners, that is due to the pressure he shoulders in being the eldest and only son of our family. He takes his responsibility and duties very seriously, especially when it comes to engaging in business dealings for the family company. But Edwin has a soft heart and a special devotion for those whom he cares deeply. I have noticed that warmth when he talks about you."

"He talks about me?" Charlotte's narrative was becoming more startling.

She nodded her head gleefully. "When he told me everything that you had done in helping me come through my illness, I noticed the fondness in his eyes and admiration in his tone of speech. The day Edwin came to speak with you, I asked where he was going, and I perceived he was determined to visit you. By his nervous cues, I assumed he was going to express his feelings that day, but he obviously discerned it was not the right time to carry out that conversation."

Her explanation ended with that statement. She mirrored my silence which allowed me a moment of peace to wrap my mind around this new development. "Honestly, Charlotte I do not know what to say about all of this."

"You do not have to say anything." Charlotte reassured me. "You have shown yourself to be open with me in our friendship, and I wanted to imitate that by discussing this with you. I know that you are a determined person Adelia, and I thought that bringing this to your attention now might make you receptive to the idea of Edwin's desire to court you in the future."

"It is a delicate subject to consider." I sighed.

"Well, we do not have to discuss it again, unless you want to." She smiled comfortingly. "And you should know, I will always want to be your friend, even if you are not interested in forming a close relationship with my brother, whether it be platonic or romantic."

"Thank you, Charlotte." Her kind words made me feel better about the future of our friendship. I looked at the clock nestled on the fireplace mantle, and I realized it was time to depart if I was going to make my 2 pm appointment with the solicitor.

Now I had something else to mull over in my mind. I contemplated all that Charlotte had said as I sat in the carriage for the short drive to Mr. Wilson's office. She had told me Edwin had never met a young woman like me. *"I do not believe I have ever witnessed a young woman act as you did"*. His words echoed in my headspace. When I had brushed off his statement, telling him all women are perfectly capable, he had tried to affirm me further, saying, "*You have most certainly demonstrated that for me*". Had he really been trying to compliment, maybe even hint that he had feelings for me? I had barely taken notice of his social cues or expressions that afternoon, which is highly unusual for me, as typically I am alertly observing and studying how people interact with me.

"Are you alright Adelia?" My aunt's voice pulled me out of my musing.

"Yes, I am fine." She must have noticed my quietness.

"How was your friend, Charlotte?"

"She was well." I smiled. "We talked for a little bit; it was a pleasant visit." I gave her my nondescript answer and then was silent as I had run out of words to say. One situation at a time, I told myself as I stepped out of the coach with a thudding step, almost if trying to stamp out all of my unresolved issues entirely. I needed to get through this meeting! After that, I would have plenty of time to ponder over and debate this new disclosure regarding Edwin to the fullest extent possible.

"Miss Hadlee, there are several things to consider regarding your late father's assets." Mr. Wilson responded to the question I had posed about why we were sitting in his office discussing my father, a subject that seemed irrelevant.

"That does not make sense to me. If I had any inheritance at all, why would I be finding out about it now? He died when I was quite young." I spoke with confusion.

Mr. Wilson's bushy mustache twitched in equal confusion. "Miss Hadlee, when do you believe your father to have died?"

"The last memory I have of my father is when I was a small child and then everything else regarding him is blank. Most of my childhood memories consist of my time living with my aunt and uncle. They adopted me because both of my parents had passed." I felt my face flush as the room was painfully quiet. I turned and looked at the two of them. "Is what I said correct?"

"Yes." Uncle Richard spoke and my confidence rose. "Mostly." It plummeted back down with that one word.

"Whatever do you mean?" Everything was now decidedly disconcerting.

Aunt Leah sighed and leaned forward. "Adelia, after your mother died we were all in a state of grief, but it hit your father the hardest, understandably. I was always involved in caring for you, a role that I enjoyed greatly. When the time came, your father made the difficult decision to hand you over into our care."

"Then my being adopted was not the effect of my father's death? He willingly abandoned me?" My voice faltered as I stammered. "But whenever I asked about him as a child... when did we have a miscommunication on such an important detail?"

"Adelia, we were not ever exactly sure when your father died. After your mother Jolee died, Charles threw himself into his secular work, which included traveling abroad. Eventually, all communication ceased from him, and he would not return our correspondence. We assumed he had passed away, either at sea or in a foreign country." Aunt Leah explained.

"It was practical for you as a young girl to steadily live with close family members who could provide constant and quality care. Leah was your mother's sister and we all agreed she was the best woman to have a motherly influence on you." Uncle Richard softly stated.

That was certainly true in my case, but I was completely derailed by the fact that my father had been alive much longer than I had originally believed. I was having trouble moving forward, and Mr. Wilson seemed to notice, which led him to continue the formal conversation.

"On the subject of your father's travels, we have much to discuss regarding his business endeavors." Mr. Wilson briskly spoke.

I pushed aside the brewing thunderstorm of emotion, reminding myself I could sort out the details with my family later in private. "Yes, what about my father's business connections abroad?" I said while taking in a deep breath.

"Well, the bulk of the matter lies in these documents and proceedings." Mr. Wilson opened a marginally thick sienna folder full of crisp white papers covered with dashes of black print. I scanned the documents with my eyes as I listened to Mr. Wilson talk about my father's business connections and I observed my father's signature scribbled on each page. Charles Beckham. The name felt foreign on my tongue. I had grown up a Hadlee, under the care of my aunt and uncle. But I was also a Beckham and seeing my father's scrawly signature pushed that fact forward into my mind.

"Mr. Beckham traveled to several countries searching for a business connection. He eventually settled a company in India." Mr. Wilson told me.

"He founded a company in India?" I inquired. A peculiar tingling feeling flew up my spine.

"Yes." Mr. Wilson confirmed while glancing at his pocket watch. "Mr. Beckham became partners with another businessman he met in India. What was the family name again?" Mr. Wilson started rustling through the papers rapidly. "I have asked the current partner of the business to meet with you today so that you can become acquainted. You will be working with each other in the foreseeable future." A strong knock resounded on the closed door. "Ah, there he is now. Two thirty exactly! Come in."

I do not know who I had predicted to walk through that doorway, but I definitely had not been prepared to see that familiar pair of sparkling sapphire eyes gaze into my dazed and befuddled face.

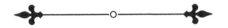

Chapter 11

"Miss Hadlee." Edwin addressed me formally with a slight bow.

I was too shocked at his presence to remember to curtsy. "Why are you here?" I dumbfoundedly asked.

Mr. Wilson quickly replied. "Mr. Castelow is here to represent the other half of the business, Miss Hadlee. Are you two already acquainted with each other?"

We both voluntarily ignored that question. It was glaringly obvious to everyone present in the room that we had some sort of history together, the way the two of us were looking at each other, eyes locked, both trying to desperately figure out this confounding situation.

"How long have you known about this?" I finally spluttered, annoyed that he possessed knowledge that I was not privy to. He seemed suspiciously unfazed by this current turn of events.

"I did not know anything at all about your involvement with this." Edwin said defensively, refuting my claim. "All of the paperwork that directed signing over the company to the heir, listed that person as a Jo Beckham." His eyes darted to the desk, scanning over the mountainous mess of documents, and seemed to pick out a particular piece of paper. Pointing to a black scribble of a name, that was carefully printed at the bottom of the sheet, he handed it to me. I glanced at it and started to smile as I realized that my father had dictated my name in the document to be written as Jo Beckham. It had made the name ambiguous; no one involved in the company's affairs would have had thought that the new owner of the company was female.

"Yes." I looked up at Edwin. "I am Jo Beckham. Jo short for Jolee, my father apparently used my middle name in his legal documents."

"Ah, a strategic move for the company, by Mr. Beckham. I believe most everyone assumed I was going to be meeting a Joseph Beckham today." He told me with an amused smile. "So, as Mr. Beckham's daughter......" Edwin paused, his gaze looking past me, intently studying something in what seemed to be a faraway scene in his mind. "Adelia Jo Beckham." I heard him faintly whisper my name, still focused on a distant place, not in the present. I was about to ask Edwin what he was doing when he snapped back to attention.

Mr. Wilson spoke in an attempt to get the meeting back to focus. "And this would make you the majority owner of fifty-one percent of the company, Miss Adelia."

It was a puzzling amount of information to take in over a short period of time, so I sat back down, subtly introducing Edwin to my aunt and uncle. He said hello while smiling and then looked back at me. I consciously avoided making eye contact with him again. I had come to recognize the expression his face softened into whenever he was in my presence, ever since that night I had saved his sister. This detail lined up with the narrative Charlotte had explained earlier that morning, which caused apprehension to sink into my heart. I instantly wished that Charlotte had never told me details about her brother that were now manifesting in front of my eyes. Each glance, every word from him, made me now wonder about the possibility of Edwin being fond of me, and I did not want my thoughts to be distracted with the idea of that subject.

My arms had somehow crossed over and into themselves as I shifted in my chair, and my aunt looked at me curiously, observing my change in posture. I smiled slightly at her sweet face, to reassure her, and through the simple glance exchanged between us, I knew we would be having an interesting conversation later that evening.

The meeting continued, and the rest of the time was spent discussing the company affairs and my role in the business. As I now owned the dominant share of the company, I was going to be playing a significant role in managing the business alongside the Castelow's. I learned through Edwin that he had taken over the main role of the executor for representing the Castelow's side of the business this past year, with his father stepping in or assisting when needed.

Basically, our fathers had somehow met in India, formed a friendship, and eventually became partners in their business, which is known as Beckham and Castelow Shipping Purveyors. The history of the company showed a proven track record of successful profits, and it was explained to me that this was a result of the business being founded as independent from other major British shipping companies and our fathers only seeking out quality product suppliers that paid their employees fairly for their labor. The company had been able to gain a firm foothold on textile, spices, and tea exports, back when these business relations were not strongly established yet in India. The business had an exceptional reputation for treating employees and customers well, which helped with business endeavors, and also made me feel a sense of pride in my father's accomplishments. I was most surprised at how lucrative the business was, and my eyes widened as I examined the figures put in front of me. Mr. Wilson informed me I was quite the heiress now, with about 7,000 pounds a year, along with the additional wealth of my initial inheritance from my father.

Now that all of these details had been piled upon me, the meeting ended, and I quickly thanked Mr. Wilson, before taking my leave from the cramped, stuffy room. I was walking out with even more questions than before the meeting had begun, fearing that I may never receive sufficient answers to said questions. I heard my aunt and uncle still talking to Mr. Wilson, as I stood in the hallway, where I could view the doorway leading out. Seeing the bright light outside seemed to attempt to help clear the cloud of feelings floating over my head. I now heard Edwin in the other room, saying goodbye to my family, and then in a few strides, he was in front of me.

"Hello, again." He gently smiled.

"Hello." I said simply, still staring out into the doorway.

He stayed by my side, even though I was distracted. "How are you doing with all of this?"

"It is an inordinate amount of information to process." I sighed and looked up at his face.

Edwin nodded. "And how are you dealing with your father's passing?"

"I do not know." I answered, growing agitated, not at him, but at the question. "I feel as if I should be feeling something, something more. But I keep asking myself, how do you grieve someone you barely knew?"

He studied me closely, listening to me intently. I thought I could see concern reflecting in the pools of blue that were his eyes.

"I was raised by my aunt and uncle." I explained. "That is why I prefer to be called Miss Hadlee. They are the only family I have ever truly known. I obviously do not know all of my father's story, and it is frustrating trying to figure it out."

"I cannot imagine how difficult that would be." He replied and I felt as if the weight on my shoulders was lifted a small amount now that I had vented to someone about my frustrations. "Your father was a kind man. He was the initial force behind insisting employees of the company be treated fairly and paid well for their labor. And of course, he was always thoughtful when it came to Charlotte and me. He would take the time to speak with us when he was doing business with my father. He was a good man. I am truly sorry for your loss Adelia."

I realized he probably had more memories of seeing my father than I had ever had. It stung to dwell on the fact that my father had been alive for so many years, but for some unknown reason had not chosen to spend time with his only child. A pang of sadness threatened to crumble my composed posture, but I bit my lip and looked at my feet, telling myself I could fall apart later when not in the presence of Edwin Castelow.

"And I now can see from whom you inherited your green eyes." I heard him say.

I rose my head back up to him, hoping he would not see the tears brimming in my eyes. "What do you mean?"

"Your father had green eyes just like yours. They are a gift to you from your father."

I knew in the recesses of my memory I could conjure up a memory of what my father looked like, but it felt so hazy in this moment. Edwin sharing me this detail about my father made me so happy. "Thank you." I whispered, a smile playing on my lips.

"You are welcome." He smiled in return, content that my smile had decided to spread across my face. "I want you to speak with my father sometime. He was close friends with Mr. Beckham and might be able to tell you more details about your father or stories you have not heard yet."

"I would like that very much. Thank you."

"Well, you and I will be continuing to work together in the future. You might as well become closely acquainted with all of my family." Edwin said teasingly. "My father will probably be there at the next business meeting when you are introduced as the new company owner."

"I am looking forward to it, then." I told him. At that moment, my aunt and uncle came out of the inner room and walked towards me.

"Goodbye, Adelia." Edwin said in an undertone to me, and then with a respectful nod to my family departed from the building.

We left as well, and I was more than relieved when we arrived back at Helena's house. I quietly retired to my room to collapse on the bed, the day's events leaving me with a feeling of enervation.

Later that evening, I stood in front of the mirror with a candle in my hand, peering into my own set of eyes. Edwin was right, my eyes were a shiny dark green, the color resembling the pines of an evergreen forest. I could recall people in the past telling me that my eyes were brown or almost hazel, but I now envisioned my father's face as I closed my eyes. He had dark hair and a trimmed beard that I used to burrow my little fingers into when he held me. I easily pictured his smiling green eyes, laughing as he swung me around, me giggling, the whole time wrapped in his arms. How old was I in this memory? I could not remember, but to know that I shared the trait of green eyes with my father somehow comforted me.

"Can I come in?" I opened my eyes and saw my aunt standing in the doorway as I had left open the door to my room.

"Yes, please do." I began to braid my hair while watching Aunt Leah sit down on the bench at the end of my bed.

"How do you feel about what you learned today?" She asked me.

"I am alright. How old was I when my father gave me over to you and Uncle Richard?"

She took a breath as she thought. "You were about four or five."

"So, if he went to India, I could understand why he was unavailable when I was younger, or why I was unable to come with him." I began to walk the length of the room, rambling and my tone rising. "But where was he all of those other years? Why did he not wish to see me?"

"Adelia, do not view it like that. Your father must have had an exceptionally good reason for the way he navigated through life."

"How else am I supposed to view this situation? He knew where I was, he could have contacted us, or me, but he chose not to." Sadness crept back into my faltering voice. "Please do not think that I am saying I am unhappy with being in your care all of this time. I do not want you to believe that at all!" I exclaimed with frustration, confused as I tried to explain myself. "What kind of person does not want to know their own daughter, their only child?" I had now stiffly stomped over to my bed and buried my face in my pillow to hide the red anger blooming on my face. I laid still, inhaling the crisp cotton smell of my freshly laundered pillowcase.

I felt my aunt squeeze my arm gently. "It is going to be alright, Adelia. You must remember how many times I have observed that you are an identical resemblance to your mother, Jolee. Each person deals with grief in different ways. Having a spirited, beautiful daughter that reminded him of his late wife each day may have proved exceptionally difficult for your father." She smoothed my curls back from my forehead as I continued to take smothering breaths into my pillow. "We will have to keep asking questions. What about his business partner? Maybe they would know more about your father's whereabouts."

I lifted my face from my pillow. "Yes, Edwin told me that his father might know more. Since our fathers worked together, maybe Mr. Castelow would have additional details that could be shared."

"That would be interesting. Hopefully he will have something enlightening to tell you."

"Edwin said that he would be at the next company meeting, so I will know soon enough." I had flipped onto my side, resting comfortably on the soft quilt, thinking about how lovely it would be to go to sleep. My aunt was suddenly quiet though. "What are you thinking about?" I asked as I opened my eyes and saw her watching me.

"You and Edwin are fairly familiar with each other? I hear you are on a first-name basis."

She was right, I had referred to him twice as Edwin in the last sixty seconds, and she must have heard him call me Adelia earlier.

"We have become friends in recent months. If you remember, he is Charlotte's brother."

"Yes, I do remember." She smiled, and I was wondering if she was going to ask to hear more details about Edwin. "I am glad you have them. You need to have good, true friends in your life."

"Well, you are the truest friend of all." I said, throwing my arms around her. "I am going to miss you immensely." I told her, holding on tightly to our embrace so I could remember the warmth and love that I felt when I was near her. My aunt and uncle were leaving the next morning, and the thought of not having my aunt to physically talk to each day made me feel disheartened.

"I am going to miss you too, dearest. Are you sure we should not stay longer to assist you if needed?"

"No, you do not have to." I would have loved for her to stay into perpetuity, but I knew that was not possible. "I am going to have to figure out how to run a business without major assistance eventually. Besides, I know how the ailing population of Hastings clamber for your attention."

"Well, I wish you were coming back home for a visit. The cottage does not feel the same without you." She said and I could hear that her words were tinged with sadness.

"Thank you for telling me that, and I too miss those merry days and memories at Cliffside." I leaned against her shoulder. "But I feel like this is where I am supposed to be right now. I have a new purpose and motivation in my life."

"Alright, but always know we love and miss you. Even though it might be a confusing and difficult situation with your father, there are exciting happenings you can be looking forward to as well." She smiled, and I could feel how happy she was for me. "Did you ever think you would be the majority owner of a company?"

"No." I said. "No, I did not."

However exciting it initially felt to know that I owned a company, I also knew that becoming a businesswoman in a society ruled by men was going to have its own challenges. Edwin had informed me that several other men who are involved with the company's suppliers in India were going to be present at the first business meeting I was attending. According to Edwin, they now knew there was an heir for the role of the business, but he had refrained from informing them that I was female. We had both decided it would be better for this detail to be an unexpected revelation. I stood in front of the humungous mahogany door, bracing myself for whatever bias might be awaiting me on the other side. As I reached for the doorknob, my hand shook, and I felt irritation at myself for just how truly nervous I was. I had every right to be here, as I was my father's sole heir. But in my heart, I knew the majority, if not all, of the businessmen on the other side of this door, would not interpret a woman being the head of a business as a positive development. Telling myself to be as courteous as possible while relying on boldness if needed, I walked in.

Edwin saw me immediately and his face brightened. The other men who were gathered together talking turned at his expression and took regard of me.

"Miss, did you take a wrong turn? This is a business meeting." One fellow spoke.

"This is the meeting for Beckham & Castelow Purveyors of Fine Goods is it not? I am Miss Beckham." Announcing myself with my father's last name was unorthodox for me. I felt an unfamiliar rush of authoritarian energy course through my veins as I uttered it aloud for the first time. For a few moments, a deafening silence hung in the air. Finally, someone else spoke.

"Miss? Miss Beckham? We were expecting a Mr. Jo Beckham?" The man turned to Edwin, desperately searching for clarification.

"I am Jo Beckham. I am Adelia Jolee Beckham, Jo short for Jolee, and my father signed the possession of the company over to my name." I explained civilly.

"A woman as the head owner? Why would he have thought this would be a grand idea?" Another man openly grumbled.

"Mr. Beckham chose to sign the company over to his daughter." Edwin walked over closer to me. "I met with Miss Beckham last week, and the solicitor, Mr. Wilson, confirmed that all of the documentation is official and in order."

"Yes, but do you not have a brother Miss Beckham?" The insolent man addressed me again. "A man who could run this business?"

"No sir, I am my father's eldest and only child. My mother died immediately after I was born." I said, straight-faced and holding the piercing intensity of my voice. I had not been hoping to garner any type of sympathy from this man by explaining my family dynamic, I instead wanted him to feel ashamed over his ridiculous comments.

"Well, even if this is all fair and legal, surely you know you are not required to take over this position if you do not wish to." This other man who spoke up tried to exude kindness in an attempt to alter my thinking.

"And relinquish my father's legacy that he left me? No, I have willingly decided to be fully involved with the day-to-day operation of the company and the tasks that this role will require of me. Now, what is the first order of business today?" I stated dismissively.

We were able to proceed with the meeting, the men who had loudly expressed their disapproval of my position over the company were now mostly silent. Those two men, who now found themselves employed by a woman, had spoken up briefly to explain their roles in the company, and then not having anything else significant to say, filed out of the room quietly. Being glad that that confrontation was over and hoping I would not have to interact with them in person again, the meeting was adjourned. I leaned against a chair in the room for support and took a deep breath. I observed that Charlotte had also been in the room, and she rushed over to me now that I was available for conversation.

"Adelia you were amazing!" She gave me a huge smile and enveloped me in a warm embrace.

"I am obviously not following the conventions of what a modest and composed woman should be, but I could not help myself." I explained the dauntless attitude that I had portrayed earlier.

"You are the owner of the majority of the company, so they should have treated you with more respect. It should not matter if you are a woman." She gave me an encouraging smile. "They are going to see that you are a force to be reckoned with."

"I would agree with that." Edwin said while approaching, coming over to stand behind his sister. Charlotte purposefully glanced at me, her eyes subtly pleading for me to observe her brother's attitude toward me.

"Oh, look who is eavesdropping on conversations now?" I lightly mocked him, trying to ignore Charlotte's reminder of a subject that I was still avoiding in my mind. "I am glad to see you here Charlotte, we have not talked in a while."

"Yes, I said I wanted to be here today in order to see you and provide support, and my father allowed me to come." I now focused on an older gentleman approaching us, and as Edwin and Charlotte smiled at him, I realized this was their father.

"Adelia, this is our father, Benjamin Castelow." Charlotte introduced me and I respectfully curtsied.

"Miss Beckham." He spoke. "I am sorry for the loss of your father. He was a good friend and will be dearly missed."

"Thank you." I swallowed, unsure of what to say next. It left me with a hollow feeling when others spoke about the absence of my father. My father had been missing from me for as long as I could remember.

"Edwin told me that you are struggling with missing knowledge of your father's life. I am sure I could explain a few things, but for the most part, Charles was a private man. I think you would learn more from this." He handed me a leather-bound journal, wrapped with cord, and full of jagged papers, spilling out of the seams. I took it in awe, wondering what discoveries I would find in this book. The hope of the words recorded in this book providing any degree of clarity seemed the most appealing.

"This is wonderful, thank you." I said, expressing my appreciation. Mr. Castelow spoke kindly to me, and I could see the same energetic glimmer in his bright blue eyes that Edwin had inherited from him. Mr. Castelow was similar in height to his son, and his hair being fully grey contributed to his distinguished appearance, looking the part of a wise father who had experienced many things in his life.

"The journal was on your father's desk in his office, which is now your office. I figured you might want to have access to it now, and I was not sure if you have had the opportunity to go through your father's personal possessions yet." He smiled. "I can see the same tenacity and resolve in you that Charles had."

"I certainly demonstrated that today." I said, secretly wondering if being fierce was going to be an asset or a complication.

"You were splendid. I am sure the company will benefit from the fresh viewpoint that you will bring, Miss Beckham. You have the ability to make a lasting impact with your actions and words."

"Thank you, Mr. Castelow, you are too kind." I breathed in again. These were inspiring words that I needed to hear in this moment. "That is very encouraging of you."

"Well, you have significantly impacted both of my children." He said and I glanced over at Charlotte and Edwin who were talking amongst themselves. "Charlotte speaks often of how glad she is that you two are friends."

I smiled fondly. "Yes, we are good friends. I am happy to know someone as gracious and kind as your daughter." Our conversation ended shortly after that.

When I retired that evening, I found myself engaged in my typical task of reliving prior conversations in my mind. It struck me bizarre that Mr. Castelow had said I had impacted both of his children. Did he also know something about Edwin having feelings for me? Had Charlotte told her parents about this potential development?

It was difficult for me to dwell on this concept without fearing the searing dread of the burn that could come if I became emotionally infatuated with someone who did not reciprocate my feelings. I shook off these trepidatious thoughts, knowing that if I continued to repress them, I could drift peacefully into a sound sleep.

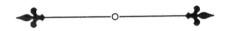

Chapter 12

I was engrossed with a flurry of tasks the next few weeks regarding the company and involving rearranging my father's possessions. There were two offices located in the building our company occupied, one for the Castelow's, and one that was now mine. I was thrilled at the prospect of inhabiting a new space, and my office area was most certainly promising. I was also implored to attend different social events with Helena and Theodore, which were suddenly exciting as I felt more invigorated about socializing with unfamiliar groups of people. Of course, the Castelow's were usually present at these functions, so I could always connect with Charlotte and enjoy meaningful conversation with her as well.

January arrived, announcing a new year, and ushering in the long, freezing wintery nights. It was on one of those icy cold evenings when I found myself at a dinner party that my cousins were hosting, laughing and talking heartily with Charlotte. As I spoke with her and surveyed the room with my eyes, the breath in my chest evaporated when I thought I saw a young man who had the same likeness as Henry Ansley. The person I had seen was standing across the crowded room though, and when I summoned a degree of courage to peek again, the figure was no longer there. I blinked the uncanny feeling away, stilling my beating heart and telling myself I had a fantastic imagination that was playing tricks on me. However, when his familiar enchanting voice resounded in my ear, I decided this illusion was either truly real or I was having an intense lifelike dream.

"Hello, Miss Hadlee." I heard him say which caused me to sharply turn my head to see his face. "I am immensely happy to see you again."

I was utterly speechless. Standing before me was the man I never thought I would see again, or if I were to, I had assumed that he would have a wife attached to his arm. With a quick scan of the immediate area, I surmised there was no Lady Monique anywhere near Henry's vicinity. I stealthily looked over at Charlotte who knew nothing of this situation or who Henry was, and her pursed lips and knitted brows expressed as much.

"What are you doing here?" I had no control over the words that slipped from my lips.

"I am visiting a few of my friends in London for a while." He smoothly explained with a beaming smile. "I heard you have been here in London these past months. I was hoping to cross paths with you."

I did not know how to receive him in this moment. I wanted to shriek, demanding him to explain his behavior with Lady Monique, who he had been close with during the summer. In lapses of weakness, I still relived that moment in my memory of when he had brushed me off at Edith's wedding, and as I stood staring at him, reflecting on the countless nights that had only ended from the exhaustion of crying over him, I grew exasperated.

"I honestly thought you would have been extremely preoccupied planning your upcoming nuptials to ever consider where I was located in the world." I huffed, temper flaring and anger coursing through my entire body.

The expression on his face sobered, a hint of remorse reflecting in his dark eyes. "Yes, well Lady Alarie and I were never truly engaged." He shifted uncomfortably on his feet, and I felt my muscles relax. "That situation was contrived from our parents trying to encourage a connection between the two of us. We parted ways amicably, and I have to say, I continued to think of you Adelia, even while I was being entreated to pursue Lady Alarie and long after you left for London."

I was so caught up in my emotions that I could hardly gather my thoughts. He was never engaged; he was claiming his feelings had been with me all of this time. My head was spinning and seeing the face that I had swooned over for almost a year of my life was not helping the situation. Then, to make things more complicated, Edwin walked up to us, smiling at Charlotte, and then confusedly observed me standing mutely alongside Henry.

"Adelia!" Edwin said brightly with a smile. "It is good to see you tonight." He stepped closer between Charlotte and me, glancing over at Henry to acknowledge him. "I do believe I have yet to meet you?"

"Oh yes, this is Mr. Henry Ansley, an acquaintance from Hastings." I spoke up hurriedly to explain. "Mr. Ansley, these are my friends, Miss Charlotte Castelow and Mr. Edwin Castelow." With proper introductions having taken place, the conversation ensued, with me asking Henry after his family, wondering about Clara, Oliver, and Edith. Charlotte and Edwin stayed close next to me, carrying on their own conversation with another person whom they knew. I noticed Edwin continually glancing over at me, observing my interactions with Henry.

In the span of a few moments, the room started to close in on me, the laughter and chatter assaulting my ears, feverish heat washing over me as I grew more uncomfortable. When Henry attempted to ask me a question about the recent turn of events regarding my father's estate, it all became too much to contend with.

"I am sorry, please excuse me." I suddenly muttered, trying to breathe through my mental suffocation, a heavy weight bearing down on my chest.

Henry stepped aside to let me take my leave, and I vaguely recall him saying something else to me as I walked away, but the sounds in the room had mixed together reverberating as a harsh cacophony in my ears. Desperately searching for a breath of fresh air, I wandered to the next room over, maneuvering myself between the circles of people in my frantic movements, almost tripping over the edge of my long dress. I spied a pair of identical doors that were slightly open, so I covertly crept over to them, hoping no one would notice my departure. The opening led out onto a lengthy terrace, and I stepped out under the gracious canopy of the night sky and twinkling stars, sighing in relief at the welcoming desolation and solitude the fresh night air afforded me.

I stood with my fingers clutching the edges of the frigid railing that was standing guard around the upper balcony. Crisp night air infiltrated my lungs, giving me renewed breath and a spark of energy while the quietude allowed my musings to come forth. I was uneasy regarding Henry's presence in London. Enough time had finally elapsed for the wound on my heart to have healed and I had finally come to terms with what had never truly transpired between Henry and myself. Now he had surprisingly reappeared, and he had the ability to string along a tizzy of emotions that were wrapped up in me. He had been everything I ever wanted, but my ideals had drastically been readjusted. I was internally fighting between an inexplicable urge to scream out into the darkness or break down in tears when a resonant voice disrupted my bleak and panicked aura.

"Adelia." I glanced over my right shoulder to see Edwin striding over to me. "Are you alright? I brought you this." He was holding my shawl that I had left inside. He lifted the soft fabric up around my shoulders, and his fingertips fluttered against my neck, prompting a sharp inhale of prickly, piercing air to hold in my chest. Our eyes locked and a distinct hum of energy thrummed between us, enticing me to become lost in this surpassing moment.

"Are you cold?" He quietly asked.

"No." I replied. A blush had diffused a radiant warmth over my entire being as I stood inches away from him. In the past, I had always turned away at the intensity of his ardent stare. Right now, I was spellbound by his sapphire eyes, a striking color I had only ever seen in beautiful stained glass.

"Adelia, I noticed that you became distressed." He put his hand near mine, our fingers resting side by side on the terrace ledge. "Is there anything I can do to help you?"

I delicately shook my head. "I believe I would benefit from the passage of time, Edwin. It has been said that time cures all wounds, and I have to allow myself patience to process the consternation that the past brings forward." I explained while staring out into the darkened horizon. The stars had been covered with a blanket of clouds, bringing shadows to the already inky night sky.

"Adelia, you were there for me when I was despaired over Charlotte being unwell. You saved my sister from illness that could have taken her from me. I am forevermore indebted to you."

I was transported to that night we had cared for Charlotte. After her condition had improved, Edwin focused on me, noticing I was fatigued and insisting that I rest. His expression then was full of protection and care, the same attributes that he was displaying for me in the present moment.

"Please, always know that I am more than willing and eager to assist you in any way possible." Edwin finished declaring his resolve.

"Thank you." Gratitude struck my soul as I thought about his words. "I am appreciative for your reiteration of a determination of loyalty to me. Loyalty is a virtue that I have come to deeply admire in a person."

His eyes were focused on me, sparkling behind two sets of thick, black lashes, hypnotizing me with each steady blink. "It comes naturally for me to show my loyalty to you, Adelia."

We stood together on that small balcony; my heart being opened two-fold by the man standing before me. Crystals of snow began to dance in the air, and a shimmering beam of moonlight decided to slice through the clouds and shine down on us, setting a whimsical atmosphere. I wanted the image of Edwin, in this moment, to be fixed permanently in my memory, in the same way the intricate snowflakes were gently clinging to and melting into his dark ebony hair. I let myself truly acknowledge his physicality, detecting in myself a hint of attraction as I memorized the outline of his face. I wondered if I could sketch the lines of his subtle square jaw, elongated nose, and dimples that contoured his face when he smiled. A simple graphite sketch would disappointingly not be able to capture the bronze tone of his skin or the blue jewels that are his eyes. I dared myself to look him directly in his eyes again, and I wondered what thoughts he was pondering as he returned my gaze. Silence was enough for the moment, and an unseen magnetic force pulled me closer into him, our fingertips meeting, snowflakes kissing our faces, each of our breaths exhaling as frost.

No matter how many times I tried to conjure up the image of Edwin in my daydreams, I could not replicate the exact feelings that he had evoked in me, on that fateful evening, one week prior, standing on the darkened terrace of the Braxton residence. His presence sometimes seemed to stimulate a degree of familiarity in the recesses of my memory, a sentiment that had continued to haunt me since our first unexpected meeting. That night when he stood with me, I felt that I was on the brink of illumination as I studied him, but the revelation was lost when he had beseeched me to come inside due to the inclement weather. It was as if I was enjoying reading a novel, and then I discovered the last chapter was full of blank pages. Wishing to discover the lost words that had mysteriously disappeared from the story, I anticipated a future opportunity when I would find myself in his company once more.

One morning while sitting in my office, a knock at my door proceeded to make my day more interesting. I bid entry while standing up and smoothing my skirt, and then I was unduly surprised with a barrage of flowers being escorted through my office door. The arrangement was so massive that I could barely make out the profile of the delivery man from the florist shop. When placed on my desktop, the array of purple violets, red roses, and pink lilies took up almost half of my workspace. Their vibrant hue reflected in my vision and the deliciously sweet fragrance made me dizzy as I picked up the card with incredulity, wondering who had sent this elegant arrangement of flowers to me.

Dear Miss Adelia,

It was my fondest desire to deliver this gift to you in person, but I was called away to attend to a most urgent matter. It was a pleasure to reestablish our acquaintance at the Braxton's party last week. It seems that I will be staying in London for an indefinite period of time and I am anticipating the pleasure of calling on you to enjoy your company and further affirm our acquaintance.

Affectionately,

Henry Ansley.

I sighed, resting the card against the flowers, and gently leaned against my desk. My first coping instinct regarding Henry reappearing had been avoidance, thinking if I could evade his physical presence, the emotional presence of him would release itself from me as well. Attentions from him such as these flowers were not helping to further my strategy. Being in Henry's company was the opposite of reading an unfinished book, instead, I was turning over the well-worn pages once again, reawakening the past feelings and emotions that I thought had been finalized with the close of an abrupt last chapter. My temper tended to instinctively harbor spite towards those who had caused me pain, but in regard to Henry my emotions seemed to become like a crinkled autumn leaf, succumbing to the stormy breeze that commands where it will go.

I was reflecting on the past though, and I now recognized that the hold Henry had once held over my person had greatly shifted from the time that we had spent apart. I did not have to make the same mistakes, nor dwell on them any longer. The promise I had made to myself was to focus on the future, and those around me would have to prove if they were worthy of being included in my long-term happiness. Satisfied with that determination, I started to rearrange the scattered items on my desk that had become displaced by the flowers. I was soon startled by a second knock, and I glanced up to see Edwin standing at my office door which had been left open from the flower delivery.

"Hello." I smiled, happy to see him, this being our first meeting together after our shared moment under the night sky on the terrace.

"Hello, Adelia." He greeted, his mouth mirroring my smile. "I had some business matters to attend to at the office today, and I was hoping to find you here."

"Well then, I am glad I was here to be found. Please, come in." I beckoned him to enter, and he walked towards the center of the room. I watched quietly as he studied my office space, taking in the changes I had made to the furnishings, and then his eyes settled on the immense vase of blooming flowers resting on my desk.

"That is an impressive array of flowers you have there." He said with surprise, and his eyes darted through the different flowers, processing what the meaning of each of them could be.

"Yes, I suppose they are." I replied, not wanting to discuss anything remotely related to Henry Ansley with him.

"Are they a gift of well wishes from family?"

"No." I purposely stepped in front of my desk to cover the card when I noticed Edwin trying to glance at it discreetly. "They are a gift, sent by an acquaintance."

He paused, clearly thinking about what he was going to say next. "Is Mr. Henry Ansley sending you correspondence?" He finally asked, confirming that he had read the signed name on the card.

I glanced back at him pointedly. "Edwin, surely you did not come to see me today in order to converse about my personal interactions with someone else?"

"Well as your business partner, I am of course naturally curious about any matter or correspondence that could potentially concern my business partner or myself." He replied with a tone of nonchalance.

"I do not think a vase of flowers that Mr. Henry Ansley sent me would cause you any reason for concern." I said and then looked at him again. "Or would it?"

"Oh." He broke his gaze, in an attempt to conceal the blush creeping up his face since I had caught him trying to unnecessarily inquire about my relationship status with Henry. "No, it certainly would not."

I purposely stayed silent for a moment, forcing him to start the conversation again. "On the subject of gifts, it seems that I was not the only one who had that idea in mind. This is for you." He brought his hand forward, extending a rectangular shaped gift box to me.

"May I open it now?" I asked, my curiosity thoroughly engaged, my hands eager to open a gift from him.

He nodded and watched intently as I unwrapped the packaging to gaze upon a small cedar box that revealed a gift of an ink pen set for writing.

"Thank you. This will be excellent for writing and signing business documents." I delicately closed the wooden box and then noticed an engraving that I had overlooked when I first opened the case.

Abhita

Passing my index finger across the inscription of letters, I tested the word on my tongue, realizing that it was a name, a name that I somehow knew, foreign as the pronunciation sounded against my ear. Edwin had purposely given me the gift with this name engraved my intuition was telling me that this name referred to my past.

"What does this name mean to you?" I looked up at him with incredulity, and he shyly smiled.

"It is a name of great importance." He started. "Quite simply, it is your nickname. When I met you at the train station that one day last autumn, your presence piqued something in me. The curls framing your face, fierce green eyes staring up at me, your determination to release yourself from my grasp, vaguely evoked something deep in the recesses of my memory, even though I did not recognize you at first. I was desperate to learn your name, in hopes that it would give me a measure of peace from the mystery that you had become in my mind. When I was formally introduced to you, the name Adelia was extremely reminiscent, but it was finally resolved when I learned, many months later after our initial encounter at the train station, that you are Miss Adelia Beckham."

"Yes." I said memories and images starting to rush forward. "Our fathers knew each other; they were business partners."

"And you and I used to know each other." He finished for me. "One summer when I was about seven or eight years of age, my father would allow me to accompany him when he would go on business trips down to the ports in London."

"I can recall meeting you." The blissful childhood summer was freely coming forth now. I could see the younger version of Edwin, same dark hair, deep blue eyes, shyly glancing at me, eventually smiling, and then running to catch up to me as we explored.

"Charlotte was an infant at that time, so I did not yet have a sibling who I could play with, and I always eagerly looked forward to seeing you when my father would take me to the shipping warehouses."

"I believe the sentiment was mutual. You easily made me laugh and were always sharing your toys and games to keep us occupied." I told him, remembering stealthily hiding behind shipping crates, waiting for him to find me, and colorful marbles or pebbles that we would toss and swirl on the floor.

"I remember you would bring a book with you sometimes." He said, touching a stack of novels I had recently acquired and placed on my desk. "I would sit next to you, and you would share with me, the two of us turning the pages and staring at illustrations."

I silently smiled, lost in awe that all this time we had a hidden connection that traced back to our early childhood.

"But the most memorable attribute about your younger self, Adelia, was your fearlessness. You would run up to the loft in the warehouse, persuading me to break my cautious nature and follow you. One time, you dashed up the stairs first and before I could stop you, you were standing in the middle of the wood plank that connected the two wooden platforms of the loft."

"I had been wishing to balance across it for a while." I told him, remembering my resolve as a young child to cross the high beam at least once. "You cautioned me not to walk on it whenever you had caught me staring at the plank."

"The height of the loft was at least one story; it could have been fatal if you had fallen. You did not have an ounce of fear in you though, instead, you walked out onto the middle of the beam and looked back at me, smiling confidently to reassure me, your unruly curls bouncing with each careful step, my fear absolving the closer you got to safety. You were almost at the other side when both our fathers walked in and observed you, teetering high up on the plank."

"They asked us to come down." I replied absent-mindedly, momentarily reliving the surge of panic I felt when I saw our fathers looking up at me standing high in the air. "We rushed from the loft, I was expecting to get disciplined for being reckless, and for you to be scolded for allowing me to get into a dangerous situation, but my father simply picked me up and with a kiss on my forehead told me he was relieved that I was safe."

"My father said you were a little Abhita, a name in Hindi that means brave or fearless. I called you Abhita from that moment forward, in memoriam of your brave act on the beam, a reflection of your childhood ability to be uninhibited and free." Edwin finished while coming closer to me, reminding me of our brief interaction on the terrace. "I still see those qualities in you today, determination, courage, strength." His hand gravitated to the pen box, his index finger tracing the engraving. "You are still the Abhita I knew when we were children."

"And after an unexpected collision and slight disagreement at a train station, we found each other again." I thought back to our first meeting as adults and how ever since then we had both felt the impact of each other, a bit of clashing tension at first, then our personalities melding into a fundamental friendship.

"I am most glad for that interaction; however brash it may have been." He said and I gave him a glance of exasperation, but he only laughed, revealing that he was teasing me.

"I cannot deny that I was perhaps somewhat audacious and curt that day, but you most certainly were bold and relentless in asking after my name." I scolded with a laugh.

"It was only because I was unexpectedly enthralled by a complete stranger, who turned out to not truly be a stranger to me after all." He explained while stepping closer to me, the expression softening on his face. I found myself hoping to observe some form of adoration, perhaps a singular emotion in his expression that he only revealed when he was near me. He had told me how he viewed me as courageous, but I wondered if he knew that when I was near him, his presence now simultaneously awakened a bubbling fierceness and wild weakness in my heart.

Instead of figuring out how to articulate these sentiments to him, I settled on a rather mundane and vague comment. "We certainly have enough history together to form an excellent business partnership."

Edwin agreed with me. "It will be enjoyable to see what the future holds for the two of us, considering how well we got along as children."

"Yes, it shall." I said, still actively absorbed in the fact that all of this time we had pieces of each other scattered throughout our collective memories.

After an additional few moments of talking, Edwin said farewell, and as I watched him leave I surprisingly found myself wishing we could have continued in each other's company, entranced in conversation the rest of the afternoon. With this new revelation about the two of us sharing childhood memories, it now became apparent that Edwin could also be a vital link to assisting me in unlocking distant memories and lost details of my childhood relationship with my father. Naturally, as business partners we had a professional relationship mapped out in front of us, but I could also detect a small spark of headstrong affection that was ignited in my heart, struck by the unlikely match that I had found in Edwin Castelow.

I sat back down at my desk, the midday sun reflecting gently on the grand arrangement of flowers on full display in front of me. I picked up a pen from my new set, balancing the weight between my fingers, and began to write on a blank page, the dark ink swirling into curves of letters, my mind preoccupied with the exciting happenings and events of the past few months of my life. I used to occupy my days with planning an ideal future, hoping and dreaming that everything would perfectly fall into place. As of late, my life seems to take unexpected turns and directions, as if I had gained passage on a ship without a compass, with the wind and waves as my true North instead, directing the final outcome of my travel destination. I now embrace the unknown, basking in how free I feel as an individual, excitedly awaiting the marvelous discoveries and new experiences that await me on the distant horizon.

The End

Made in the USA
Las Vegas, NV
08 November 2021

34026503R00105